RESURRECTION MILL

Pete K Mally

Edited and Typeset by Wrate's Editing Services, London
(www.wrateseditingservices.co.uk)

Printed and bound by CPI Group (UK) Ltd, Croydon, CR0 4YY

To Ruth Cope

Acknowledgements

Thanks to Grant Lorimer, Patrick Norrie, Andy Gibbons, Chris Crooks and Ian Russ. You have all inspired me with your talents. Thanks also to my family in Dundee and Down South, to Danielle Wrate, and to everyone else who had to put up with me spouting on about Geordie Mill.

PROLOGUE

18th JULY 1823

The Howff Cemetery, Dundee, Scotland

Derek McCaw kept his hands in his pockets and his collar up over his neck as he thought about those privileged few enjoying their evening tucked up in bed in the prosperous Perth Road, overlooking Magdalen Green. He was headed the other way, north of the High Street, towards the Howff cemetery. Once, it had served as a combination of a meeting place and burial ground. Seen as safe haven for all, the town's Incorporated Trades meetings had been held there. People did their business and paid their respects to the deceased. Now it was simply a graveyard, its high walls designed to keep the bodies in and the criminals out. Derek walked through the slightly open gate and gave a subtle nod as he passed two burly Charlies standing rigid in the cold night. The rain was relentless and the darkening evening sky reflected his melancholy mood. He pulled his collar up further, sheltering his stubbly face from the large droplets falling from the Scottish skies.

"Evening gents, you would never guess it was July, would you?"

"Right enough, Mr McCaw," said the larger of the two watchmen, "even the weather's given up on us."

"Aye, it has indeed. Well, I hope all is quiet tonight."

As he spoke, Derek made his way past the ornate gateway towards Barrack Street. He pushed his hands deeper into his pockets, protecting his balled-up fists against the cold night air and his defeated mood.

"Don't you worry, though, Mr McCaw," shouted the smaller of the watchman as he turned the corner, "we'll look after them all right. We'll keep our precious ones safe, won't we, Freddie? We'll make sure those bastards don't disrupt the dead. God bless their souls."

"Aye," Freddie replied loudly, for Derek's sake.

Derek heard the watchmen's dialogue and normally he would have appreciated the gesture. However, deep in his soul he knew it was futile. Absolutely and utterly futile. He thought of Margaret, his wife. If she knew what he was about to do he was certain it would be the end of her. *If poverty or disease didn't get them, heartbreak would,* he mused. He'd watched their son, Jimmy, as he died in Margaret's arms, observing the watery diarrhoea, the vomiting and the pain on that small, innocent face as the boy's muscles cramped up in his legs and lower back. Watching the life pour out of his body as he was torn inside out by such a vile, putrid entity was bad enough for Derek and his wife, but the thought that those bastards would then steal his body for some posh lecture hall in Edinburgh was enough to drive Margaret mad. Derek realised that he needed to take charge. He needed to do *something.* He couldn't save his boy's soul, but Goddamn he could save *his* soul. The idea had come to him as his son lay on the cold floor, his bluish skin tight and stretched from the invading disease, his mouth still open, a little vomit on his bottom lip. He knew if he didn't act he would regret it forever. Looking at the image that would forever be etched on his mind's eye, he made a pact that *no one* would use little Jimmy McCaw, his six-year-old babe, as an exhibition to those toffs whose parents had paid for their spoilt upper-class brats to dissect the bodies of the young and innocent to further their so-called education. Anatomy? Butchery more like.

At the boy's funeral earlier, a crowd had huddled behind him and Margaret. Derek remembered thinking how she had never looked so old, so frail. The small, cheap wooden coffin was placed gently into the ground. Derek knew that the body of their son would already be decaying inside it. He was one of the many thousands of victims of the evil scourge of modern-day sickness. As Margaret had swiped another tear from her face one more immediately replaced it. Derek, once again, formed fists in his pockets, but this time he had cut into his palms with his fingernails. He'd be damned if he would let his wife see him weep. He needed to be strong. As the pallbearers placed the earth onto the miniature coffin, Derek knew what he had to do before the rain packed down the soil.

Once home, Margaret had cried herself to sleep. Derek had slipped on his long jacket, gently closed the door behind him and walked back to the cemetery, knowing that Alistair and Fred would already be on guard. They were the local watchmen, or Charlies as the press had recently named them. There were over 100 names on the watchmen list. Men of all ages and sizes had volunteered for the job, but there always seemed to be the same two on sentry duty night after night. Derek understood why this was. His own name was probably on that list somewhere, written in a moment of defiance to the body snatchers. When he'd signed it, he supposed he had every intention of doing a shift or two. But that was before cholera had gotten hold of his only son. Everyone knew the pressure these watchmen were under, due to the uprising in bunking, but that didn't stop the wrath of the public and the anger towards them when the grave robbers succeeded in their plunder. Tower or no tower, lookout or no lookout, if the body snatchers got their loot the watchman would be target practice for the baying mob. Derek realised it was a very unfair state of affairs.

He had consulted with Alistair and Freddie shortly after the funeral, in a quiet spot under an oak tree, while an exhausted minister consoled his wife. He told them of his idea, reluctantly at first, but with more confidence when they didn't interrupt to protest or show contempt, as he had feared they might. As each man held his hat in his hand and looked firmly at the ground below, Derek laid out his plan. When he had finished, the men both nodded in agreement without raising their eyes (they were both hardworking fathers after all), but they insisted that Derek would have to be the one to take action, because if they tampered with the coffin they could find themselves being accused of bunking. Grave robbing watchmen? Sadly, it wouldn't be the first murmur of it happening. The three men were more than aware that murmurs usually led to lynching. Derek agreed to their terms – it would be a solo act.

Now it was 4am, and the funeral felt like a lifetime ago. The rain had temporarily stopped – a long overdue break – but the ground was still soft as Derek dug into the moist earth with the old, stained spade he had retrieved from behind the small watchtower. The half moon shone down on him as he stood, spade in hand, in a trench, digging down until he reached the wooden coffin that just twelve hours earlier had been lowered with the blessing of the minister. With an almighty heave, he opened the coffin lid and a loud creak broke the silence. Derek looked inside the wooden carton, which was the part he had been dreading most. Thankfully, the smell was no worse than he had imagined. He tried not to look at the deformed face of his lifeless young son lying there in his Sunday best. Wiping a tear from his eye, he opened up his canvas bag and pulled out a collection of wires. He tied them around the sides of the coffin and around Jimmy's body. Squatting now, he clipped each wire into place with putty and pushed it gently against the wooden sides, using his thumb and forefinger against each other. Cautiously, Derek took another smaller bag from his larger one, unclipped it and began to prudently pour its contents around his son's head. The gunpowder lay in between his ears and the coffin walls, but some scattered over his child's face. Being careful to avoid the eyes, mouth and nostrils, Derek continued to empty the bag. As the rain began to fall again, he gently placed the empty bag back into the larger one and returned the coffin lid, cutting off the few loose wires underneath it with an old pair of pliers. He then carefully placed the pliers and the wire cut-offs into his canvas bag. In the darkness of the night, Derek was sure the grave robbers wouldn't see his booby trap. Wiping a dirty hand over his face and removing his cap, he quickly said a quiet prayer and began the job of placing the earth back onto the coffin. As he worked, he occasionally looked over his shoulder in case some of the newly-appointed Dundee Police Force saw the movement or, even worse, members of the general public. They would almost certainly take him for a grave robber. Things were so bad that people often decided to take the law into their own hands, and the last thing poor, suffering Margaret needed was a lynch mob tearing her husband from limb to limb.

After twenty long, dark and cold minutes, Derek flattened the earth and placed the spade behind the nearest gravestone, so the watchmen could find and remove it as soon as he signalled to them. He looked again at his son's gravestone, which read:

Sacred to the memory of James M McCaw, aged only six years. He died of Cholera, 13th July 1823. This monument is erected by a few of his numerous friends, as a mark of their affectionate regard and esteem, and of the deep regret they felt at his untimely and sudden death.

Derek placed his cap firmly on his head and walked back the way he came, clutching the bag slung over his shoulder tightly as he climbed over the cemetery wall. He whistled as he did so, giving Alistair and Freddie the signal to keep a steady watch now that his vigilante act was complete.

Derek walked home through the cobbled streets of Meadowside. He quietly let himself into the house, took off his dirty boots, placed his jacket and hat onto a chair, shoved his bag under the table so the evidence could be removed the following day and let out a large sigh. The he got into bed next to his sobbing wife and gently held her hand below the bed sheet. When sleep finally found him, Derek dreamt of opened graves, of resurrections, of walking skeletons and of decaying flesh. He dreamt of baying mobs and diarrhoea, of disease and the destruction of flesh. His nightmares had become as dark as the world outside.

Before morning came, he was awakened by the noise of a loud blast.

"What was that, Derek?" asked Margaret, wiping her eyes, "it sounded like an explosion. Was it the factory?"

"Nothing, dear, go back to sleep," Derek replied as a tear rolled down his dirty cheek and onto the pillow below.

PART ONE

Extract from *The Aberdeen Journal,* 1st JULY, 1824:

Like Glasgow did twenty-four years ago, the City of Dundee has established their own Police Act. This Police Act finally received the Royal Assent. The Act should establish a notable increase in crime prevention and has been partnered up with the opening of a new jail. This Police Act will enforce law and order from the Eastern side to Mayfield and the Western section to the Blackness Toll. From Clepington in the North to the River Tay itself being its Southern boundary.

At ten o'clock every morning, a Police Court will sit, establishing a regularity of judgement much missed in this troublesome time. Judges and the citizens alike are men of good standings and of solid common sense. The Court will also house the Provost, the magistrates, the Dean of Guild and a sheriff.

The system itself is still in fluidity, but it seems that petty offenders will be imprisoned for up to sixty days and fined up to five pounds, with more serious offenders being held in the Dundee jail until the next Court hearing.

The watchmen, or Charlies, will still be prevalent, however, as they have been criticized for only attending the beat of their ward, the Police Act has assured they will compensate for this. With the increase of violent crimes, robberies and grave robberies, the decision to employ a more professional holistic system has been welcomed by the working men and women of Dundee.

CHAPTER I

CRAIG BOYD AND Graham Whyte sipped their ales and watched the distinguished gentleman raise his top hat, exposing his thick hair and protruding grey sideburns. He bowed with exaggerated gusto to the petite blonde lady, by whom he was completely mesmerised. She giggled and bowed herself, exposing her cleavage a little more, although it could be noted there was very little left to be further exposed. Then she scuttled off with her fellow lady friends to the corner of the Eagle Inn, one of the newer drinking establishments in the area of Broughty Ferry. The men glanced at each other briefly, took another large drink of their ales and continued to watch as the man straightened his hat, stroked his collar, dusted down his large, black jacket and strolled confidently to the bar area, a look of self-satisfaction evident in his slightly drunk, crinkled face. He got himself a dram and winked assuredly to the barman.

The men's viewpoint, at a side table near the back of the pub, was perfect for enjoying the entertainment of people watching. They observed as crows may watch a cat pounce upon a sparrow, admiring the cat's confidence with the knowledge that it was soon to be broken and scattered to bits - sparrow's wings will always overcome the feline's brain.

The two men knew how the trap worked. They had seen it, and many adaptations of it, hundreds of times over. And they were sure they would see it a hundred times more. It was a simple scam, but it was also a timeless one. As long as there was hope in the world, there would be scams. This one involved one old, rich man and one beautiful, young lady with many friends - ladies *and* men. The ladies drinking liquor in the tavern watched the merry dance take place, the men outside in the darkened alleyway waited for their young, pretty friend to come out arm in arm with her catch. The poor gent would then be beaten and battered less rich.

Boyd and Whyte continued to admire the view of this all too familiar scenario as the dram was drunk and the woman walked over. Then, like clockwork, off they went, arm in arm. There came another wink to the barman from the elderly gent and another wink from the woman to her friends, who were obviously as well trained in the scam as she was. It seemed to the two men that everyone in the damn tavern knew the only outcome of this scenario. Well, everyone except the elderly gentleman. He pushed open the tavern door and out they went into the cool night.

Whyte and Boyd found that all the hustle and bustle of Broughty Ferry came to life in the Eagle Inn. They watched the young dockworkers who were there to flirt with the young female patrons, the men who were drinking away their wages with a new Indian pale ale, the men who had been expected home three hours ago and the men whose habit for whisky ruled their habit for living. Cholera wasn't welcome in these places, they were only for people enjoying their hard-earned cash. Well, them and the occasional plague of rats. Boyd drained his tankard and Whyte looked at his watch and smiled at his companion. He knew what his friend was thinking. It would happen soon. Just like clockwork. The commotion would ensue in no more than six minutes. They gave each other another smile, placed their empty tankards on the table, along with some money for refills, and carried on their short conversation, all the while knowing it would soon be interrupted by broken bones and broken pride.

"You think it'll work, then?"

"Aye, course it will, Craig," Whyte replied. "He'll be thinking how in a couple of minutes he'll be balls deep, when in fact he'll be up shit creek with a boot to the face, an empty wallet and nae fuckin' paddle."

The thin barmaid with the deformed right hand that resembled a talon slammed down two more tankards on the table next to them. Rumour had it she'd had her bones crushed by a horse when she was young. Others said she was the daughter of a witch. Whyte tried not stare at the claw/hand and instead focused on the beers replacing his cash... the cash that was disappearing quicker than a rat down a cellar. He was pretty sure bar work wasn't the woman's main source of income, but he couldn't quite remember her story. He would ask Craig later after this scene played out.

"This here honey trap, Graham, is pretty common, right? But people still buy it every time. I mean, Christ, this new police force has got a job on its hands."

"Craig, *we've* got a job on our hands. I mean, we start on Thursday."

"Ah, I ken, Graham. Just you know..."

"You're no having second thoughts are you, Boydy? I mean, three pounds a day and we get some action, tae. Let's face it, these bloody Charlies are no working. They've the best intentions an all but the bastard burkers are outsmarting them every bloody night. Soon they'll be nae bodies left in the ground, ken what I mean?"

"Eh, I ken," replied Craig, taking the first gulp of his drink. "I'm just a bit worried. What's happened? Dundee used tae be so nice an all."

"Dundee was never fuckin' nice, Craig. You ken that."

"Aye, suppose so. But have you heard about that killer down in Edinburgh? Killing people with arsenic in their bloody snuff. The world's gone fuckin' mad, Graham."

"It's always been mad, Craig, it's just popping its ugly heed up above the parapet now. You know who I blame? Those bloody smartarse doctors who insist on cutting up bodies. You ken what I mean? And the arseholes who pay to go see these smartarse doctors cut up these bodies. What's the world coming tae, Craig?"

"Aye" Craig replied, enjoying his drink. The world was suddenly all right by him. It was Graham's round next.

"I mean," Graham continued, before taking another gulp, "no medical students, no demand for dead bodies. No demand for dead bodies, no burkers. Am I right?"

"Aye," said Craig, who was getting thirsty now, "that's all in Edinburgh, though."

"Yeah, but here's just as mad, Craig. I mean, there was near a fucking riot last week in Long Lane Cemetery when two burkers were caught with spades in hand. There was another beating of a Charlie who failed to retrieve the body of a five year old that went walkabout from a grave. It's going fucking mental. On Friday last, a group of thieves tore the padlock from a spirit cellar in the Vault. The same evening, Craig, Horse Wynd's cellar was broken into just after the Barrack Street shoemaker got robbed with a false key."

"Aye."

"I mean," Graham continued, now obviously on a verbal roll, "remember last month when these pickpockets got caught in the act and were dragged by their necks by the crowd to the jail house? Y'ken what happened after? When they were confined in the jail house some bastards stripped clean their Blackness Road house of any valuables."

Graham took a breath and began again, while Craig looked

dejectedly at his empty glass. "And then there was Perth last week. Three men jumped that woman on her way to Lochee. They stole her basket and twenty-five shillings. The same day there was a robbery in West Port and hemp and yarn was nicked. I mean, what can you do, eh? The public still think there are four watchmen in the High Street, Craig, but they can only afford to pay for two of them. I mean, their beat is from the bank at Castle Street to the English chapel at the Nethergate, right? So, when the New Inn Entry was robbed, what could they do? Abandon their beat and get sacked from their subscribers? I mean, it's the subscribers that pay the watchmen's wages, right. So, like it or not, they make the choices. Try telling the public that, though. My mate says he's just back from Edinburgh where a Charlie was pushed out of a watchtower at New Carlton Cemetery by two gravediggers. Broke his fucking collarbone in the fall. They seem more successful, I reckon, than here."

"Aye," Craig agreed but said nothing else. It was still Graham's round after all. Maybe silence would give him the hint. He hoped it all wouldn't kick off before Graham put his hand in his pocket.

"It's worse in Glasgow, though. Remember that Bridgeton shambles? It was in the paper. When that poor family opened up their son's grave in John Street Cemetery to add their younger one, they found the body was gone. They ended up all going around with pistols and swords, and a poor wee bastard shot himself. I mean, he was only seven. These gravediggers are a problem y'ken, but you don't tell a seven year old to load a pistol and join a burker hunt. Least he shot himself clean in the head. No suffering, I heard. Dreadful, though."

"Aye, Dreadful."

God his throat was parched.

"So," Graham concluded, now well and truly on his soapbox, "I mean, just look around this neck of the woods. You have these crazy bastard Polish gamblers who have joined forces with the protection racket from Lochee. You know the guy who was found in the Dockyards that night with a screwdriver in his head? He lost the card game and didn't pay enough winnings, I heard. Then there's that bloody Geordie Mill, Gus Liffie and William Walker who are always up to some sort of dodgy shit. Chancing bastards, the lot of 'em. Hopefully, they'll all kill each other off. And that's why, Craig, it's up to people like us. Citizens are now joining the law. The ones with moral fibre, a good heart and ..."

"... And a dry, parched throat."

"What was that that?"

"Eh, nothing," Craig conceded as Graham continued without a breath, " ...and a sense of justice and pride to join this new force. Dundee is not going to go the same way as Edinburgh and Glasgow, pal. We'll make sure of it. Right, Craig?"

"Eh, right," Craig muttered. He was beginning to accept that he may already have consumed his last drink when the door swung open and an elderly man came in. Craig noted he was hatless. He was also slumped over and blood dripped from his lips. One of his eyes was already beginning to swell. In fact, his face looked like it was ready to explode. A tooth fell to the ground as his voice boomed across the pub, immediately quietening the chatter.

"They robbed me. The thieving bastards robbed me! Let's get them. They'll still be outside. Come on, I need you all, guys. Let's get the bastards!"

The shouting was met with silence. Then, after ten or so seconds, the usual noise of drinking, clattering and chatting continued.

"I'll get the ales in, then," Graham said, as he made his way to the bar.

Finally, thought Craig. Then he smiled as he realised that the old man wouldn't be able to wink for at least a week or so.

CHAPTER II

"GOOD MORNING, GENTLEMEN, not only those of our dearest city of Edinburgh, and not only those of around Scotland, but indeed those from farther afield. What an honour indeed it is to be standing here in front of you all. The Lord himself created the world and all who lives in it. He built the skies, the trees, the rivers, the oceans. But his greatest achievement was the making of mankind."

Paul McKeany sat at the back of the grand lecture theatre at Barkley's School of Anatomy watching this altogether pompous performance with a mixture of disgust and jealousy. With the Royal College of Surgeons just around the corner, McKeany, not for the first time that year, wondered why Edinburgh had all the luck. Dundee, on the other hand, his home, seemed to have none of it. None at all. *Training to be a man of medicine was difficult enough,* he mused. *But practising in a city where the docks took priority and the jute mills dominated, well, it simply left no room for the academics.* In Edinburgh, it seemed, a bright mind could flourish. He reluctantly watched the confident figure of Doctor Robert Knox swan around the stage. With him was a dour assistant and they were presiding over a table covered with a pile of sheets. With a swirl of his cloak, Dr Knox continued his preamble.

"So you see, citizens, as God made man, the study of the human anatomy surely must provide a direct insight into the mind of the maker himself."

Upon concluding his speech, Dr Robert Knox indicated to his assistant, a skeletal man with too much hair and proportionally large eyes, who, in McKeany's opinion, needed a damn good scrub. He promptly pulled the sheets off the table, exposing a corpse. McKeany could see that the man, who looked like he had only recently died and was in his mid to late twenties, had a particularly muscular body, despite being slightly overweight. Even from his position at the back of the hall he could tell it was a damn fine specimen. He admired the muscular legs, the large solid chest. Perhaps he'd over indulged in a little too much rich food, or perhaps he'd gone on too many visits to the alehouses, which had given his stomach a swollen look. The early signs of gout could be detected in the feet and he had bruises on his left arm. A recent struggle, perhaps, or maybe the man had been making money as a prizefighter. After a second look, McKeany dismissed this idea. The nose appeared unbroken and there were no indents in his cheeks or eyes. Perhaps he'd been a dockworker or a sailor. There was no sign of malnutrition or any serious external injuries. The body was simply a perfect specimen.

With a large sigh, McKeany held his chin in his hands and hoped the students around him wouldn't see his look of despair.

He had travelled all the way to Edinburgh to see how the experts were doing it, but the journey hadn't been easy. He'd taken the coach the hundred or so miles and it was an experience he did not relish repeating the next day, but needs must. The carriage had contained a collection of nervous travellers whose eyes scanned the scenery intently. It was a sign of the times, a reflection of the growing number of robberies on the road, the emergence of highwaymen, the increasing murder rate and the plague, which was travelling from person to person and destroying as many young and healthy people as it was old and already dying.

Experts? The word rattled around McKeany's head as he

watched Robert Knox examine the dead specimen. When the press dubbed them 'experts' they meant that no one else in Europe matched their expertise in human anatomy. But McKeany thought that Knox and co were experts in one thing, and one thing only. Making money. Considering how much the tickets cost for this lecture theatre, they were making *a lot* of money. This was his second autopsy in two days and they had indeed cost him an arm and a leg. So much so he hadn't even been able to smile at his own pun.

Doctor Alexander Munroe's autopsy the previous day at the Royal Society of Surgery had focused on the dissection of an elderly man who, despite a broken leg and a slightly twisted back, was again a good specimen. *The less said about the humourless Dr Munroe, the better*, McKeany reflected. He was a very serious man indeed, and his loud, booming voice echoed through the lecture hall, obscuring the sound of the cracking of bones. His large, bulky figure and his mean eyes meant that his own assistant was visibly fearful of the practitioner. McKeany had sat through the gasps and cheers from young medical students as Munroe hacked into the shell of the elderly man who was lying, without dignity, on the slab below him. Between the two doctors there had been a possible audience of five hundred medical students. But the two doctors, in Mckeany's opinion, didn't know their arse from their elbow. Or, indeed, their femur from their fibula.

McKeany continued to watch as the more flamboyant Knox swirled his arms in the air, pointing out the heart, kidneys and liver. *Even his apron*, McKeany mused, *was clean*. The audience was made up of rich medical students and some wealthy but bored middle-aged men. They were all wowed by the performance that was more like a Shakespearean play than an autopsy. If Knox was Prospero doing his magic with Ariel and Miranda to impress, Munroe was Shylock retrieving his pound of flesh.

"Blood, guts and drama," McKeany said quietly to himself. "It shouldn't be about the drama, it should be about the *body*. He looked around at the excited faces of the audience. They were grinning and smiling, mouths open with wonder.

McKeany had seen enough.

Half an hour later, as he wandered about the impressive grounds of the Barclay's School of Anatomy, he pondered the noises and images from the autopsies. But these soon faded as he reflected his own position. He himself could do, if not a better job, at least one that was the same standard as these two sought-after celebrities. He simply *knew* that to be a fact. He strongly believed that his knowledge of the human body excelled most, if not all, other people's, and that his ideas about systems and the mechanics of each part of the body and how it influenced the other had great merit. He just needed to *show* this skill and prove that his knowledge was second to none and revolutionary. He needed to *show* Scotland and the rest of the damned world that he, Paul Samuel McKeany, would change the way the human body was considered and studied. He would dismiss the theory of 'bad air', 'miasma' or 'night air' that these so-called experts believed to be the cause of disease and put forward his alternative – that some may soon call the *McKeany principle*. This principle was based on the *correct* idea that it was *not* the air but something in the flesh itself that caused these plagues, as well as the spark of an idea about how the human body creates a chain of events … so the heart's activities influence the liver, the liver influences the stomach, which then influences the kidneys, and so on.

"Sir, I want to study McKeany's Law of Spiral Anatomy," he said quietly to himself, smiling at the thought of this potential future.

Dundee hadn't a place to study, never mind an autopsy chamber, but this had less to do with a lack of intelligence and more to do with increasing the damn jute industry. But the population was growing and McKeany knew that it was what the city required: a place to study, to take the limelight away from the capital. And, goddamn it, he knew he was the man for the job. Doctor McKeany's autopsy lectures would sell out and future medical hopefuls would travel from Cornwall, Exeter and Cardiff to see the famous, skilful, modest McKeany explain the human body and structure. His theories would be widely read, his lectures well attended and, above all, he'd be *well* respected. Now that he had seen Knox and Munroe with his own eyes, he had every belief that he could do this. And indeed do it *better*.

Mrs McKeany would be so proud of him. He would finally be the husband she had always wanted to kiss and not the one she had been pressured into marrying by her father, who'd been keen to secure their social standing. *It would even,* McKeany mused, *make her more adventurous in the bedroom.* Knowing her husband was *the* name on everyone's lips would perhaps make her want to give him *her* lips.

There was just one snag. Money. He'd need money to hire a space, money to hire an assistant and, above all, money for getting the medical supplies that he'd need. In other words, the corpses themselves. What with the warm summer and the continual fog, bodies tended to last only a day or two before they decayed and maggots had their way. During both lectures, McKeany had asked himself two main questions. *Where* had the bodies come from? And, more importantly, *how* could he attain such bodies in immaculate condition? If he could figure out that, he was pretty sure the other factors would fall into place. As he continued to work through these thoughts, his successful future felt very close indeed.

CHAPTER III

HIS LIFETIME OF travel had never suited Ronan Devaney particularly well. From the green pastures of Lithgow to the dirty streets of Dublin, from the bustling ports of Aberdeen to the fashionable streets of Edinburgh, his nomadic life hadn't been a deliberate move. He was envious of the settled people who crossed his path. They had wives and families, a job they'd done for years, a house that was a home rather than temporary shelter. This time, work brought Ronan to Dublin, but bad company soon pushed him back out again, especially the bad company of the opposite sex. How the hell could he have known that these women would cross paths and all *talk* to each other, forcing him to move across the water to try and settle in Aberdeen? A new home was on the cards, a new chapter that would hopefully end in a happy ever after. But before long, Ronan found himself in an unfortunate incident involving Maggie Multrew, a pretty, fair-skinned lassie from Pitlochry, and Scottie, his fellow dockworker. Scottie was a bear of a man who was handy with his fists, a servant to the bottle and, above all things, and unbeknown to Ronan until it was too late, Maggie Multrew's father. Ronan could be forgiven for failing to make the connection, as Maggie's beautiful, delicate features certainly hadn't come from her father's side. It was unfortunate how her less than pretty father came into her bedroom while she was naked in bed and entangled around Ronan. He'd never have imagined that he could climb through a chamber window as nimbly as he could, or that he could run so fast with his feet bare and his breeches around his ankles. Fortunately for Ronan, Maggie's father was a poor sprinter. Once back at his living chambers, Ronan grabbed the money from under his bed, shoved his clothes into an old bag and without a by your leave to his dear old landlady caught the next coach south to Edinburgh, a city that was big enough for Ronan to start again. There, he wouldn't have to live in fear of the slow-witted but fast tempered Scottie Multrew catching up with him.

The journey to Edinburgh was pleasant enough and one of Ronan's fellow travellers gave him the address of potential lodgings. His spirit had finally begun to brighten again. Ever since hearing the bellowing tones of Scottie Multrew as he barged into his little princess's bedroom, causing her to immediately pull the bed sheets over her naked body, Ronan had felt in the pit of depression. But now, as the alluring buildings of Edinburgh came into view, overlooked by the impressive castle, he felt his despair lift and his jolly disposition return. When he got off the coach he walked for fifteen minutes, his bag slung over his shoulder, his neck slightly strained by looking up at the view, through the cobbled streets of Haymarket. It was then he observed the figure of a shabby, limping man coming towards him. At first Ronan assumed the man was drunk, but as they got closer to each other he saw that he was a cripple and clearly in terrible pain. Ronan also noted that the man was elegantly dressed.

Maybe these Edinburgh streets really are *paved with gold,* he thought to himself as he recalled the less-than-fortunate looking homeless cripples in Grafton Street.

As they reached within passing distance of each other, Ronan additionally noticed that the man had a very healthy complexion. He was clean shaven, had dark, short hair and bright, brown eyes. The shabby invalid had transformed from a threadbare old man to a healthy thirty year old in a matter of a few paces. Indeed, he was the healthiest cripple Ronan had ever laid eyes on.

"Excuse me, sir," said the fresh-faced gentleman in a clear, crisp Edinburgh accent. His lilt was softer than the accent Ronan was used to up the road in Aberdeen. He stopped and leant carefully against one of the street lamps. "Can you tell me where I can find Princess Street? I have been wandering for a good couple of hours and, as you may be able to see, I have just twisted my ankle and it's awfully painful."

The voice seemed so melodic and gentle that Ronan asked him to repeat himself.

It's like being read to as a baby in the cot, he thought to himself.

The man calmly repeated himself, pointing in the direction of his left foot to emphasise his injury.

"I've just come from that direction myself," Ronan replied, pointing behind him. "It's around that corner and about another ten minutes' walk away at most. Will you be okay?"

The man smiled at Ronan. It was a genuine smile that showed off a bright and full set of teeth. "Oh, I'll be fine, thank you. It's just a bad ankle, nothing to worry about. You're an Irish man, I hear? Well, thank you, fine sir."

The man leant forward and shook Ronan's hand. His handshake was firm and Roman thought he detected the scent of soap and possibly a touch of fragrance.

"My name is Mr Wilson and I wish you a good evening," he continued. Then, as if he had just recalled his caveat, he asked, "Do you by chance like the luxury of tobacco, Mr …?"

"Devaney," replied Ronan removing his hand. "Why of course. Who doesn't, eh? Apart from women, alcohol and snuff there aren't many luxuries in this world. And tobacco will get you into less trouble."

Mr Wilson laughed. "A wise Irish fella indeed," he said.

He plucked from his jacket a little wrapped up piece of

tobacco. "Take this for your trouble, Mr Devaney. I have a lot more at home, so please, I insist."

"But…"

I insist Mr Devaney. It takes a fine-mannered gentleman to enquire about a limping old man. Ronan took the small pile of snuff and beamed at the man he had randomly but fortuitously encountered. "Thank you and have a good evening."

"Oh, I will," Mr Wilson replied.

As he walked towards the station, he turned his head and added, gently mimicking an Irish accent, "and top o' the mornin' ta ya. Good luck."

Ronan had a large smile on his face as he held the small, wrapped up package of snuff in his hand and carried on towards the lodgings that had been recommended to him. He didn't believe in omens and, unlike his sister, he wasn't of a superstitious disposition, but he felt that finally there was an angel on his shoulder and Edinburgh was going to supply him with the new, settled life he longed for. Thoughts of Maggie and her red-faced, angry father soon disintegrated like sand in the wind. Things were indeed going to work for him and maybe, just maybe, he had reached his final destination, his happy ever after. He opened the packet and took some of the tobacco out with his left hand, pinching it between his thumb and index finger. He then placed it on the back of his right hand and inhaled deeply. It was a dry tobacco, finely cut. Immediately Ronan felt even brighter than he had done minutes previously. His mood had well and truly crawled from the pit and it felt as if he was floating to the clouds above as he continued walking.

John Wilson watched as the Irishman took the snuff. Now Ronan wasn't the only one smiling. John Wilson's limp quickly began to peter out before finally fading to nothing and being replaced by a fair, steady stride. And why shouldn't he walk with pride and glory? After all, he was doing God's work, wasn't he? The Lord himself had bestowed on him the heavenly responsibility of being his own right hand. He knew this as clear as he knew his own name. He, John Wilson, had been born with a special talent indeed. And this talent was recognised by the Lord above. Yes, indeed it was. There was a guaranteed place in heaven for John Wilson, but first he had to do the job that God Almighty had trusted him to do. He had to finish his mighty fine work. He considered the lowlifes that made up the working classes: the dockworkers and the prostitutes, the whalers and the shoe shiners. He thought about the new licensing laws and all the sin and debauchery they had caused on the Scottish streets. Mr Wilson knew he was chosen above these wretches who called themselves human: the ones with pitiful lives, dirty existences and deplorable cravings for sin and disrepute. They were shambolic excuses for existence.

Reaching four was a good milestone, but by the end of the winter he hoped for the figure to have risen to the 20s. There was no place for the burkers or the rapists in Heaven, but there was a place for John Wilson next to Jesus Christ himself, if he continued ridding the world of these disgusting vermin who had the audacity to call themselves men. He didn't do this to make money or gain sexual pleasure, as that would be a sin. He simply did it because he knew he *should*. God *wanted* him to do his work. He *needed* a man on the ground – a foot soldier. His smile continued as he thought about getting home and mixing more of his expensive tobacco with arsenic powder, which he could then generously hand out to the vermin who'd made his land so utterly filthy.

*

"What the hell's happening to me?" Ronan wondered as he crawled along the street. His knees scraped along the ground and his eyes bulged from their sockets. His throat felt as if it was being squeezed. Things were so tight he could have almost drowned in his own spit. As blood poured out of both nostrils, he attempted to vomit, only he couldn't open his swollen throat wide enough. It wasn't long before Ronan stopped wondering as death moved in to soothe his ungracious agony.

CHAPTER IV

A S THE DOOR slammed shut into its wooden frame, Charlotte McKeany sighed. It was a deliberate exhalation that could clearly be heard in the adjoining room of the large Brook Street lodgings she shared with her husband in Broughty Ferry, Dundee. He was home after four days away. They had been four peaceful, calm days in which she had read, sewn and not had to dodge uninvited, wandering hands at every turn. Charlotte was ashamed of her husband's thin and gangly physique, but the fact he had the sex drive of an adolescent boy who had discovered his first pubic hair drove her to distraction. He never gave up trying to woo her into actions in the bedroom, telling her tales of his colleagues and their wives, lovers and even their students. It was futile. If Charlotte wanted to make love to a fork she would damn well make sure that there was a very tasty piece of tenderloin at the end of it. The thought of sexual intercourse with that man, that twig-like creature whose talk consisted either of flattery and courtship or the bloody organs of the human body made her feel queasy. His clothes covered him like a sack and his glasses, which were perpetually smudged, gave him the appearance of a skinny youth caught in the act of masturbation by his mother. She let out another sigh, just in case the first had fallen on deaf ears. It was fair to say that she was not best pleased that he had returned from his trip from Edinburgh. Tales of dangerous highwaymen, burkers, murders and mayhem in the capital were on all her friends' lips. So why, if these were true, couldn't his stay have been extended by… well… by forever? *It wouldn't be a problem,* she thought to herself as she heard him remove his outer coat and throw his bag on the floor. *She* would *cope.* Her father would keep up the rent for their two-bedroom abode. As the sitting room door opened, she wondered once again why she had married at all. Of course, she kept up the pretence that one day they would have children. As things stood, she just might if that meant never having to see that twig-like man's naked features again. Looking at him in a state of undress was like witnessing a sapling growing its first pathetic bowed branch. *Why* did she marry? Oh, who was she attempting to fool? Her father, Dr Fairborough, had insisted upon it.

Doctor Fairborough was the smartest man Charlotte had ever known. He was intelligent, muscular and always busy, well groomed and polite. Women loved him and men wanted to be with him and, as a child, Charlotte had been the proudest pupil in her class. Her contemporaries seemed only to have violent fathers who drank and smoked. As she had grown up, the feeling of gratification over having such an accomplished man as a father had grown with her. So, when Dr Fairborough recommended Dr McKeany as a man of means, Charlotte was happy to oblige. After all, her father had simply *never* miscalculated, and Charlotte's dream was to make him proud. Occasionally, when some naughty but normal teenager feelings crept up on her, she fantasised about moving to London and meeting, then marrying, Captain Fitzroy, the adventurer and master of the seas. Now here was a man in her father's mould; the type of man she deserved to be with. She recalled her father reading about him in the newspapers, telling her, as she sat on the chair next to him, about his adventures and his courage, the way he showed the savages compassion, religion and the way of the British Empire. Instead, here she was with Mr Paul McKeany, a teacher to a few keen students who had more money than sense. Tall, lanky, short-sighted, horse-faced McKeany, who, in a matter of minutes, would ask her to come upstairs, telling her that he had missed her when he was in Edinburgh and that he would soon be the most famous anatomy teacher in the whole of Scotland. Blah, blah, blah. He would then sit next to her on the bed and slowly move his arm across her shoulder. At this point, Charlotte would make her excuses, claim that dirt and pollution from the city was affecting her head and visit the bathroom. The situation was more than familiar and, frankly, she was more than a little bored of this dance of evasion. Where was Captain Fitzroy at this moment? Sailing around the world on his ship, no doubt, mastering the rough, wild waves like no man had done before him. He was most probably shouting orders to his subordinates, with no word of complaint or thoughts of unfairness as the torrential rain pounded his muscular torso. *If only God had made more men like that,* thought Charlotte, as she stood up and walked up the stairs to the bedroom. At least pre-empting the move would save them both some unnecessary dialogue. McKeany followed and Charlotte's fantasies of Captain Fitzroy soon disintegrated as he entered the bedroom chamber and placed his wet cloak on the bed. He then slumped down next to it and produced a sigh as big as the one his wife had made two minutes earlier.

McKeany sat down and turned his head, clocking Charlotte glancing at his wet clothes over the neat bedding. Her eyes were glaring as if a party of children had just stomped their muddy boots all over her clean house. She *was* beautiful, though, that was undeniable. Her large, almond-shaped eyes, slightly upturned nose and flawless pale skin were framed by a head of shiny, brunette hair, which curled at the sides, giving her the look of an expensive porcelain doll. McKeany was an expert in the human physique and Charlotte was the best specimen he had ever encountered. After wooing her and her father, he had finally managed to marry this delightful young woman. It was just a shame that the feelings weren't mutual.

His initial thinking was that it was simply nerves. Charlotte was always under her father's gaze, always trying to impress the stern man. But McKeany had realised on their wedding night that his new wife, although spectacularly exquisite, lacked a certain...personality. He felt that if he became the lead anatomical teacher in the country, with students coming from far and wide just to see his incredible lectures, Charlotte would begin to see him differently. Her father would be so proud of his son-in-law and, of course, so then would his wife. And those feeling of pride may well breed *other* such positive emotions, perhaps more carnal ones. He allowed himself to think of things to come as he gingerly removed his hand from his knee and placed it on Charlotte's, who was now seated on the bed next to him. It had been a long journey to Edinburgh and back, but his exhaustion melted away as he told her about the lectures, the styles of Knox and Munroe and his dream to be better than them by becoming more popular and precise than the two showmen. He told her he would soon be the best anatomical lecturer in Scotland, possibly the world. He then slowly lifted his hand from her knee and placed it on her shoulder.

Charlotte promptly stood up and went to the bathroom.

CHAPTER V

G EORDIE MILL WIPED his stubbly face with the back of one of his large, dirty hands as he finished his strong, hoppy ale. "God bless the man who made this shit," he muttered to himself as he put down his jar of McEwans Indian pale ale and reached inside his large brown jacket for his packet of snuff.

"Tobacco, alcohol and mighty fine woman," Geordie reflected. "What else does a man need? Money perhaps? Even a little fine food would do me no harm."

He also reflected how 'mighty fine' wasn't the most truthful portrayal of Rosie Trayling. But by Christ she was well endowed and knew how to show him a good time. When it was his time to leave this shit-stained world, suffocating in Rosie's puppies would be a more than adequate way to say goodbye. He sat in the smoke-filled Globe Tavern and for the umpteenth time thought back to when he first met the red-haired, wayward Rosie, who hailed from Carnoustie.

It felt like only yesterday and the memory took over his senses as it had done many times before. Back then he'd had some loose guineas in his pocket and a stirring that needed seeing to. It lingered even after he'd wolfed down a beautiful meat pie and consumed three pints of ale. The money was from a card game he'd just won. He'd taken the best coin from the sexton, Ewan Taylor (the officer of the church), and the Long Lane watchman, David Petrie. The game was called Skat, a frankly confusing shambles of a game in Geordie's opinion, but it had been introduced by the sexton who had picked it up in Germany. Well, the joke was on Petrie, Geordie reflected – he had cleared up good and proper. While the sexton would manage, Geordie knew the watchman would be in for a hiding tonight from his wife, who was pregnant and expecting him to bring home food for her and their bairn. He would now only be able to bring home half a loaf, maybe a whole one if he was lucky and got his hands on a stale one.

Geordie's sympathy was soon replaced by indulgence as he celebrated his small victory in the Fisherman's Tavern, spending his coinage on some decent beverages. Now that he wasn't hiding from the Wilson brothers he liked it down in Broughty Ferry. Not that he was scared of them, but when you owed a little money things sometimes turned sour. Rumour had it they'd picked up their stuff and gone down to Newcastle with an offer of a boxing tournament and big money in the mix. Geordie wasn't so sure. Being the toughest guys in the Ferry might not transfer so well south of the border.

"There's always a bigger fish," Geordie reflected.

His dad had taught him that lesson one day after bringing home a bag full of food. He'd placed the goodies down on the table, removed his hat and told his son he had won them from a Welsh ship worker who thought he was the toughest thing since *The Great Michael,* the Royal Scottish Navy ship that sailed the seven seas.

"Those Welshies think they're tough," his dad had said, "but I've been in Dundee all my life. I put him straight. You see, there's always a bigger fish, son."

Two weeks later, Geordie's next door neighbour knocked on the door to deliver bad news to Mrs Mill and her son. Mr Mill had been beaten up so badly that he wasn't expected to survive the night. If he did live, he would never stand again, let alone work. He'd taken a beating from a beast of a man who was described by a passer-by as 'a stranger to these parts', at least 6ft tall and built as wide as a ship. When the neighbour had left, Mrs Mill broke down in tears at the thought of her and her son begging in the street and starving to death.

Geordie thought back to how his father had clung to life for four whole days, refusing to accept sympathy, refusing to accept the inevitable. On day five, acceptance or not, the inevitable took charge and Mr Mill left this world just as angry as he had entered it.

There was always a bigger fish.

It may have been the excitement of that strange, confusing German card game or the feeling of freedom after visiting the seaside margin of Dundee without getting his nose adjusted, but as soon as he saw Rosie, Geordie knew right away he'd found his end of night entertainment. She was a one all right: a sexy, gloriously indecent, spicy and lewd lady. Her face had mischief written all over it and Geordie could tell she had a trick or two up her sleeve – or indeed down her corset. Elegant, refined and sophisticated weren't descriptions that came straight to Geordie's mind when Rosie entered the drinking den, but with plump, full lips and that full bosom, who the hell needed *elegant*? Elegant was for the underachievers. Geordie knew Rosie was the type of woman for a man of the world like him. He was a man who had blood flowing through him like gunpowder. And above all, Geordie noted, Rosie was selling her trade down in the Ferry. This wasn't the docks or Peddie Street, this wasn't where the sailors came into port to hump any old tart like a stray dog. No, this was the Ferry. This was where the *real* class hung out. He downed his drink, wiped his sleeve across his face, beamed a smile that many would regard as a smirk or even a sneer, stood up and walked slowly over to his prey, ignoring all and sundry who got in his way. The rest, as they say, was history.

Geordie never considered himself a one-lady man, but with at least four more encounters since that memorable night, Geordie was sure Rosie was falling for him. And he, of course, was beginning to get used to her. She had obviously been after a man with his experience and handsome, rugged features for a while. He assumed she'd just not been lucky enough. He reflected back to that first time behind the small dyke not five minutes' walk away. And she was now charging him less for these encounters. In fact, the last time, although brief and interrupted by a vomiting child and an angry mother, she only charged him two guineas. Erica, from the north side of the city, charged more than that and her privates were as rotten as her teeth. Geordie used to struggle to decide which smelt worse: her mouth or her crotch. He had itched for days after Erica. Both times. But now he had introduced himself to Rosie and Geordie reckoned that soon the whole works would be on tap and completely free. All the enjoyments a man would ever need…and on his doorstep. Those milky thighs and creamy calves, those lips and that great bosom. Geordie's smile widened, exposing a near full set of tobacco-stained teeth. Sex, snuff and this new Indian pale ale exported from Edinburgh. Life indeed was good. When the boys arrived with tonight's loot for him he could even afford to take Rosie out for a nice drink. He might even buy her some new clothes, something less, well tempting for other men perhaps. Or should that be *more* tempting? After all, it was important to show off what was yours.

Smiling again, Geordie forced himself to stop reminiscing about his first encounter with Rosie and the turn of events that had led him to her. He concentrated on the here and now instead. Back in present time, here in the Globe Tavern, he was awaiting the boys. He opened the lid of his tobacco tin with one hand and placed some flakes on the other, enjoying a large snort from it. It may not have been the best snuff in the world but the price was mighty fine. God bless David Petrie and his snuff habit. It was bad times indeed when you lost your money, pride...*and* tobacco.

"Evening, Geordie."

Geordie looked up to see the contrasting figures of James Jeffrey and Donald McGregor, Jamie and Greg as they were commonly known around the pubs and taverns of the east end of Dundee. Jamie was a tall, lean fellow. Standing at over 6ft tall he had a strong Yorkshire accent. Geordie sometimes wondered if the reason he had never been a victim of cholera or any other disease was because it would travel straight through him. He looked as if he may snap if he bent over. With his flat cap covering his eyes and narrow face he looked emaciated: a walking, talking sheet of paper wearing a hat. Greg, on the other hand, was a fellow Scot and was as small and round as Jamie was long and thin. A hint of an Aberdeen accent broke through what Geordie assumed was Glaswegian camouflage. His portly, pudgy figure and podgy nose meant Greg resembled a pig before slaughter.

"Just in time, lads," Geordie grinned, exposing his yellow teeth to the younger men and lifting up his empty jar, "I'll hae another one, thanks."

"Yur roond, Jamie," Greg said as he sat opposite the heavy-set figure of Geordie. They both watched Jamie walk to the bar. He looked like a stork that had just lost a wrestling match with a bear. At least the barman would see him and the drinks wouldn't have to wait. Meanwhile, Geordie sensed that Greg was nervous. He was trying to bluff a confident posture, but his snout-like nostrils were twitching a little too much.

"You look worried, Greg. What went wrong?"

"Eh ...well, nah, ah wouldn't say something went wrong. I mean, we have it here, you know ...the ..."

Greg fiddled around in his jacket pocket, his tubby fingers

resembling sweaty sausage meat. But Geordie's blue-eyed glare ensured the purse didn't leave Greg's pocket to be witnessed by the unwelcoming audience that was the rest of the Globe Tavern.

Greg attempted to match Geordie's stare then swiftly conceded defeat, looking down at his feet until Jamie came back to the table. Jamie placed the tankards down, his bonnet still covering his sunken eyes. He sat down, negotiating a route around the table legs with his lanky limbs and sitting down with his knees pressed against the underside of the table top.

Geordie noticed Greg looking at Jamie's cap and was sure he was jealous because he was able to hide his eyes. He mused that the moon-faced Greg probably couldn't find a hat big enough for that head of his. He smiled and revealed his tobacco-stained smile once again. The younger men both waited for Geordie to take his first mouthful of ale and watched as he emptied half the jar in one gulp before taking a deep breath. Following a belch and another wipe of his mouth, he focused on the younger men.

"So, what was the problem?"

"No, no problem as such, you see …" Greg muttered as Jamie hid his wincing face by conveniently lifting up his jar to cover it.

"Problem?" As Geordie's eyes widened, Jamie's jar went down. An invisible thread may have connected the two.

"Well, you see," Greg stuttered, "we waited where you said for us to wait and right enough the stagecoach did come at *exactly* the time you said, right enough. And it was the Mulgrew family and they *did* have their money in their travelling purse, like you said, and we did scare the breeks of them and they *did* hand it over."

"And …?" Geordie's raised eyebrow gave Greg the shivers.

"Well, erm …you see, eh …it was windy, and, well, a fly or something went into my eye, or maybe it was a midgey. Y'ken what these fucking midges are like, eh? Anyway I rubbed it and …"

"They saw his face," Jamie spluttered.

Greg now looked like a pig that was *being* slaughtered.

Geordie's blue eyes narrowed as he looked around the pub. The world seemed to be smaller with this news. He glanced at the two old men snorting snuff at next table and at the three working men laughing at some joke or another. The barman was wiping the bar down with a cloth that was undoubtedly adding more grime to it. Nothing had changed, the temperature had not dropped further, but even so goosebumps appeared on Geordie's hairy, thick arms.

Greg's confident tone failed to hide his nervousness as he stammered, "Mr and Mrs Mulgrew won't be a problem. We scared 'em, you see, we warned 'em off. B-b-b but the kid, that scrawny little shitbag, their spoilt rat of a child ran off. He ran off the minute I put my mask back over my face. He may grass us up, Geordie. As you know, they're building a police force, we'll, we'll, we'll b-b-be …"

"We'll?" Geordie's eyes narrowed *and* his eyebrows went up simultaneously. It was like a cold dagger to Greg's already pounding heart. He felt like Macbeth facing his wife.

"Well, my-my-me and Jamie and w-w-w-well, they may follow us and well, they know we work with …"

Greg was stopped in his tracks by the sight of Geordie Mill smiling. It wasn't a small smile, but a mischievous one. A wide, beaming, leering, smirking smile. Those tobacco-stained teeth were again giving their curtain call. Greg and Jamie dared to look at each other before looking back at their leering boss with the blended feelings of fear, anticipation and all-out confusion. Greg was pleased that Jamie shared the same external triplet of emotion on that horse-like, sunken face of his.

"Well, it looks like we have an angel on our shoulder. One who is looking after me and the two of you. You see, boys, the world *wants* us to win. Now, come on, let's solve this problem that youse muppets caused."

Jamie and Greg noticed that Geordie was still smirking but that his blue eyes had shifted slightly, to just behind Jamie's left shoulder. They followed his gaze towards the bustling bar and turned very slowly back towards Geordie. Jamie lowered his bonnet slightly, an old habit he had picked up since meeting Geordie.

There he was. Eric Mulgrew himself. He was standing in the tavern, not five metres from them. His cheeks were bright red and he looked exceptionally out of breath. As he talked to the barmaid his shoulders moved up and down like a dockworker's bed after payday. He hadn't noticed Greg and Jamie, as they were facing away from him. Jamie unconsciously moved his bonnet even further over his sunken eyes.

"When he leaves here, boys," Geordie said, his gravelly voice lowering a tad, "we'll go and warn him off *properly*. Understand? I want none of your namby-pamby shit, right? I don't want him fucking saying another word, right? The next time he sees you he should be shitting so much you could sink the Tay Bridge with it, right?"

Jamie and Greg sneaked another glance at each other.

"Right, boss," they reluctantly agreed.

Greg thought if that cap went down any further, Jamie's face would disappear from view entirely.

"Good," Geordie replied before standing up. "Well, let's go. Because lads, our man has just left!"

CHAPTER VI

E RIC MULGREW DIDN'T care what his parents thought. He'd
had nineteen years on the planet and was sure he knew the
difference between *right* and *wrong*. And by jove, he knew that
being robbed on the road from Perth to Dundee and then not
informing the newly-formed Dundee Police Force that not only
had he seen one of the culprit's faces, but he could also *identify*
them was most definitely *wrong*. In fact, it was not simply wrong
but cowardly, spineless and gutless. And Eric considered these
descriptions a crime in themselves. He knew his parents had
worked hard for their wealth. They'd taught him morals and
shown him that money should be looked after and respected
and hard work should be appreciated and prized. He knew that
with his respect for values, the right attitude and a little helping
hand, he could eventually take the reins from his father at the
jute mill and buy his house in West Ferry. He'd live there with
sweet Annie McPherson, the daughter of the revered McPherson
family, who'd made their money from the jam jar industry. They
would go on to have three, four or five beautiful, hardworking
and respectful children. He could almost see them as beautiful
toddlers with blond hair and freckles like their mother. By golly,
being weak and spineless was not a way to attain these aspira-
tional ends. Ms McPherson would be so proud of him for
fighting back and showing resistance to the vulgar vagabonds.
In fact, it was probable that Mr and Mrs Mulgrew were inform-

ing the McPhersons of his actions right now, as they were their closest friends and confidantes. They no doubt suspected that their son was sorting out the matter in his manly way. Mr McPherson would be beaming with pride about his new son-in-law's bravery, courage and pluckiness. Of this, Eric was sure.

He was so certain, in fact, that he'd run to the tavern to look out for a familiar, friendly face, or faces even, and begin spreading the word before telling the authorities. It was a good idea to speak to people first because although everyone was talking about this so-called police force in Dundee, Eric had no idea where he would find any of them. He didn't truly know if they actually existed or whether they were a myth created to prevent crime. No, he would have to find his friends first. Then they could help him decide what route to take.

Eric's childhood friends, Patrick Norrie and Grant Lorimer, spent many an evening standing at the bar enjoying the hustle and bustle of the Globe Tavern, so Eric had headed there first. When he failed to see his old pals who were, in his opinion, two of society's finest and boldest men, a sense of deep despair embraced him. Eric even heard that Grant was bound for London to work in an area called Fitzrovia. He'd been utterly confident that these fine chaps would be able to help him sort out this mess and prevent the damn bandits from causing any more damage, *with* or *without* this so-called police force. Eric didn't like the Scotland of new, what with its dangerous highwaymen, a spate of murders and those damn burkers. He would do damn well all he could to put a stop to the chaos that was emerging. And of course, he'd acquire his parents' purses back too and be viewed as a local hero. Soon, brave, young Mr Eric Mulgrew of West Ferry would be the name on the lips of every society girl. Thinking of this, his despair returned to confidence as he headed out the door while musing about his future days.

He walked across Seagate towards Jessman's Court. Grant

lived up here and if he wasn't enjoying the festivities of the tavern then he must be at home. His advice and help would indeed be comforting. Eric was sure Mr McPherson wouldn't expect even his hero son-in-law to act alone, without guidance. He straightened his bonnet and walked up the cobbled street. It was a chilly evening and the sweat from earlier was drying against his forehead and the back of his neck, causing the cold to plough through his skin.

He walked for four minutes, his nerves jangling with every step. Possibly it was the delayed shock from the robbery. Hearing a clatter to his right-hand side, he sprang quickly around before realising that no one was there. Damn it, he had to concede that his nerves were getting the better of him. Feeling stupid, he attempted to focus. He reflected how this wasn't how heroes acted and attempted to regain his masculinity. Taking a deep breath and re-fixing his bonnet, he turned the corner onto Peddie Street and stumbled over a heap of discarded clothing. As he fell on to his knees, he realised it was a discarded coat. No, two coats. Now, who the hell would leave two coats lying in the street?

No wonder people are complaining about poverty and not being able to afford food if they throw away their outer garments when they get too hot, Eric thought. *If they are leaving their clothes in the street then they must be more comfortable than they realised.*

Shaking his head at the stupidity of the poor, he ungracefully scrambled to his feet and stood up straight. As he regained his balance, he wiped down his breeks and straightened his cap once more. Then, before he could take another step, he was forcefully shoved to the cobblestones below with a great force between his shoulder blades.

His shoulder and left arm took the brunt of the cobbled road as he slammed into the ground, his palm slicing open as his hand reached out to break the fall. He watched his cap roll to one side and land in a puddle of dirty water. Then, before he even felt it, he heard the sound of cracking bone. His wet hat was obstructed by a large, dirty boot that stood on his hand, cracking his fingers like twigs in a fire. Only then did he begin to feel the excruciating pain of his injuries. A terrible, high-pitched scream parted his lips and all fantasies regarding being a brave son-in-law were forgotten. He looked up through tear-soaked eyes at the owner of the dirty boot, which was still resting on his hand. His shoulder was throbbing and his feet were still entangled with the owner's jacket. Pain thrummed through his hand as he cricked his neck and inspected the faces of James Jeffrey and Donald McGregor. The rain was sliding down their faces like thick grease from a spoon.

"Well, well, well," Jamie said, removing his foot from Eric's hand, "what have we got here?"

Eric managed to get to his knees. He held the broken fingers of his left hand with his right and bit into his lip to stop himself from screaming. Tears ran down his face, creating a thick, viscous waterfall of blood, saliva and mucus. Despite being in utter agony he allowed himself to think of Miss McPherson again; her freckled skin, her golden hair, their future together. He would be her hero. This determination meant Eric never stopped showing defiance to this pair of lowlife scumbags. As his teeth gnawed deeper into his bottom lip, it began to bleed further. The flow of blood stuck to his chin and fell on the wet cobbles below, but he forced himself to hold his head up high. He would stand up to these two with dignity and honour. He felt the shorter, fatter vagabond grab him by his shoulders and place him in a standing position, but, unfortunately, his feet were still tangled in the discarded jacket and he fell back down in a heap. Pain burst through him as if someone had used a whip to slice through his broken skin. He could hear the two men laugh as he fell to the floor, his hand throbbing, the blood rushing to his head. Eric wondered how there could be any blood left. His tears were causing a curtain in which his eyes couldn't navigate through, and he could feel himself losing consciousness. He was vaguely aware of another, larger figure standing behind the two men. He was leaning against the wall with his arms crossed. Even through the dirty lenses of his teary eyes, Eric could see the figure was smiling; a dangerous, contemptuous grin that reminded him of an animal of prey seconds before he went in for the kill. Now Eric saw that he was holding a large rock in one of his large, pudgy hands. His expression was one of a cat that had not only got the cream, but the whole bloody dairy. Eric had never seen someone look so disdainful or smug. He attempted to stand again and, despite feeling faint, he managed to get up on his feet. Ensuring his feet remained firmly secure he stood up straight. His broken hand was limp and useless and hung from his side. He used his good hand to wipe the blood from his chin with his sleeve and looked straight at the faces of his three attackers.

This is it, he thought. *Patrick and Grant will walk around the corner and take them on. Then we'll walk to the tavern and the gossipmongers and locals will buy us drinks.*

This would be the moment of Eric's life that would be continually talked about in dining halls and at parties.

"You see," Mr McPherson would say, "my son-in-law here just looked at them, told them they were vermin and saw them off. Yes, he had help from his new friends, of course, but it was Eric who was the hero of the day. The new police force caught the culprits straight away. Without Eric here, these streets would be a danger to us civilised folk. I thank God he has fallen in love with my cherished child, Angela. It's difficult to have a hero in the family but we'll cope."

Eric faced down his enemies as he anticipated the clank of two champagne flutes being brought together.

"I'm not scared of you," he stuttered. "You may think you're scary but you-you scallywags are nothing but scum. Did you hear me? You're scum of the earth. That's right!"

Once he had started there was no stopping him. "I have friends, you know. Whig friends and Tory friends alike. They have power. Power and influe…"

The last thing Mr and Mrs Mulgrew's son saw was the looming figure of Geordie Mill coming towards him firmly clutching a brick. Then the whole world went blank and his fingers were no longer sore. Mr McPherson would have to find another hero to celebrate…

★

"You killed him, you fucking *killed* him."

"Be quiet, James Jeffrey," Greg replied. "Do you hear? He's just unconscious!"

He pronounced each syllable as clearly as possible to show the world he was calm and in control. But his chances of projecting composure were as thin as Edward Mulgrew's chances of playing happy families with the McPherson girl.

"No, he's fucking not. You fucking *killed* him!"

"What, are you blind as well as dumb?" Jamie retorted as he took off his cap and clutched it in both hands, squeezing it tight. "He's a goner, alright."

"B-b-be quiet. I'm tell-tell-telling you. He's just unconscious, pal. I'm tellin' ya." As Greg's voice clambered up a couple of octaves, his pudgy nostrils flared in and out like a beating heart. "You didn't kill him, did ya, Geordie. You just, you just…"

Greg and Jamie exchanged glances and both looked towards Geordie. His mouth was still open, the sneer replaced by a large void where his tongue had trouble hiding. He was still clutching the large stone in his hand. Jamie was sure he could see a little flesh on the side of what he now viewed as a murder weapon.

Geordie's blue eyes darted from Greg to Jamie. He dropped the stone on the cobbled street below as his large jaw sprung shut.

As he looked down at the still body of Eric Mulgrew he reflected how, to the unsuspecting eye, the young man simply seemed to be sleeping on the cobbles of Jessman's Court. But on closer inspection, anyone would soon spot the thick, reddish liquid tricking from the side of his panned-in skull, flowing in between the wet cobbles and reaching his discarded wet bonnet.

"Shite," was all Geordie could say as he looked at the young boy. "Shite."

Only a matter of seconds had passed since the fatal blow but time seemed to slow. All three men were standing equidistant to the already decaying body of the son of Mr and Mrs Mulgrew in a perfect triangular formation.

"Shite."

Jamie and Greg looked at Geordie. He was their leader, their mentor: a card player, a fighter, a gambler and now a cold-blooded murderer. His lips moved slowly and his voice carried enough weight so that the boys could hear him through the heavy rain.

"Let's get the fuck out of here, boys. Now! RUN!"

James Jeffrey and Donald McGregor didn't need to be told twice. They ran as fast as their nervous, young, drunken and tired bodies could carry them, racing through the cold, dark streets of Dundee's Seagate region where families were putting their children to bed and worrying about food, disease and the next day's work. Geordie took a large breath, exhaling warm air from his nose and mouth into the polluted atmosphere. He kicked the stone to one side, glancing from side to side along the gloomy street. The pollution prevented the moon's light from shining and Geordie realised there were no other witnesses. There was no one who could pin this cold-blooded crime on the three men who had been enjoying a drink in the Globe Tavern not ten minutes ago. Geordie adjusted his gait, took another deep breath, sneered gleefully at the world around him and made for home.

"Well, hello there, Mr Big and Fierce. You trying to hide, Mr Mill of Lochee?"

Lochee? It had been years since he'd told anyone where he was born and brought up. Or maybe he had? Shit. He desperately thought back to the previous week, when he'd been boasting about someone or somewhere in his childhood. Maybe he was imagining things, going insane like those sailors did when they didn't eat lemons.

"Who's there?" he asked, swiftly turning his head to his right and then to the left. His eyes took a moment or two to focus in the dim light, but once they had he saw the outline of her body. She was leaning against the side of the grey tenement wall as bold as brass. She looked just like she had that first night, when she'd been looking for custom down the Ferry. One of her legs was straight, the other was bent behind her, her heel pushing against the grimy wall and caressing its rough texture. Her hair was tied up and even through the polluted, wet night, her make-up was visible on her face. Or maybe he couldn't see the make-up and just knew it was there... it was always there, always continually applied.

"Rosie?"

"Aye, Geordie, it's your girl," Rosie replied, lowering her leg and flashing him a smile. "You left something behind?"

Geordie thought of the sprawled-out young man around the corner, his face resting in a puddle of his own blood next to a large stone and a wet hat, blood and skin still matted to its side. He quickly wiped his hands on his overcoat.

"What?"

"Did you leave something behind, Geordie, doll?" she repeated. "You see, you look nervous."

"Eh, no, I was just with, eh... Jamie and Greg, eh? And you...?"

"Or should I say *someone,* Geordie?"

Geordie Mill's world began to crumble. It was obvious she knew what had happened. "Eh, doll, you see it wasn't me. You see it was..."

He was stopped by her slim finger, which she waved in the air like a reprimanding schoolteacher. It was a gesture that no one had dared use towards him since he was six years old. Taking control of himself once more, he let himself think.

Rosie couldn't have seen the attack, he speculated. *She never saw the laddie die. If she had she would have screamed. Any lass would.*

"Don't lie now, Geordie," Rosie said. "You might have a big..." she winked and glanced downwards, below his slightly-expanded waist, "but your brain's like a pea. I saw you, Geordie. I saw the three of you leave the Globe Tavern and wondered what my big lump of a man was up to. So I followed you and watched you all surround that poor kid. Watched as you clubbed him to death like a dog."

"Nah, it wasn't me, you see..."

Rosie turned on her heels and slowly walked away, back to where the incident had taken place. Geordie panicked. The body could have been found by now, there could be an audience. He – they needed to get out of here.

"Stop! Please," he said, the desperation in his voice cutting through the air like a blade.

Rosie stopped, turned around and faced Geordie.

"In fact, you treated him worse than a dog. Now, Geordie, I know you and you must know me by now. I saw the whole thing, and you know what? This newly-formed police group might like to know how this rich family's kid died, don't you think? And then, Geordie, well then..."

Rosie made a choking noise and her eyes rolled upwards. Then she laughed. Geordie had never heard such an evil sound in all his life.

"You wouldn't," he retorted. "C'mon, Rosie, my darling. It's me your... your..."

She was standing eye to eye with him, then she took a step back and smiled. It was the same smile he'd seen after some cheap spirits and sex, the same smile she'd worn when she saw him coming out of the tavern in Broughty Ferry and knew he would have her, the same smile she'd displayed when he'd shared his snuff after that first round of rough and ready lovemaking.

"But I wouldn't, Geordie, I wouldn't."

Geordie nearly cried with relief. He sighed and moved to hug the angel, whose carnal skills had shaken him to the core. She would never snitch.

Rosie moved backwards, out of Geordie's reach. "Because Geordie Mill," she said, still smiling. "I can now have anything I want from you. Five guineas would do nicely, thank you. Meet me in the Fisherman's Tavern tomorrow evening with it."

And with that she was off, walking as bold as brass through the dark, wet evening. Geordie watched her glide around the corner, leaving him alone in the cobbled street of Jessman's Court. His mouth was wide open, his breath leaving trails through the air. He looked back up to the hidden moon and then ran. As he sprinted through the Seagate, narrowly missing a horse and cart, he realised this was not going to be the best of days. In fact, he had one hell of a sinking feeling that things were about to get a whole lot worse.

CHAPTER VII

THE PALE MOON watched over the quiet road and the only sounds to be heard were the slow clomping of a horse's hooves and the carriage's slightly rusty wheel squealing on every rotation. With just the slightest movement of his hand, its driver was able to gently guide his horse, Shadow, through the silent streets. This gave him time to reflect on his new venture. It was nice earning some money independently from his brother. In fact, Bill O'Brien would go as far as to say it was liberating. Yes, the carriage cost a pretty penny and yes, horses were not cheap to feed, water and shelter, but if he could carry on in this fashion ferrying wealthy people on routes from Perth and Dundee, he would be a wealthy man in three or four years. He might even be able to pay off his horses and the carriage in ten or eleven months.

Bill looked up again at the moon, which seemed to be shining down on his good fortune. His brother, Eck, had warned him against such a venture. He'd told him of the highwaymen lurking on these very roads, awaiting the likes of Bill and Shadow to pass so they could threaten and steal from their well-bred cargo. He knew of this, of course, but Bill O'Brien felt lucky and as no alcohol had touched his tongue for over a month, his awareness was like a hawk. It puzzled him how these bandits could sense when he had been drinking. Was it that obvious? He continually scanned the side of the road and, up in front, the moon acting as his guide. There wasn't any movement on either side of the road and, seeing the steam rising from Shadow's breath, he decided it was time for a five-minute breather. His passengers tonight were particularly amiable, so Bill was sure they wouldn't mind Shadow taking a little rest.

"Stopping for a minute or two!" he yelled as he halted Shadow with another sleight of hand. The carriage came to a slow stop, its wheels screeching. It would take another twenty minutes or so to get to Dundee, Bill speculated. It was perfect timing. Luck was indeed on his side once again. He jumped down onto the road while stroking the side of his beautiful black horse. As he did so, the curtains flickered from inside the coach and out came one of the passengers, Mr Cuthbert.

"Comfort break," he announced as he walked past Bill and into a set of trees. The carriage door was left open and Bill checked to see if his remaining three passengers required anything. His travelling companions were Mr Cuthbert and his wife, who were visiting their cousins in West Ferry, a nervous, bearded elderly man and a middle-aged gentlemen who looked to Bill like a professor or a taxman. His clean hands and smooth skin gave the impression that hard labour was a thing for others. Bill noted that the elderly man's eyes continually darted around the vicinity. Earlier in the journey, he'd heard him talking about the sport of hanging and the public baying for blood. He couldn't understand why people loved the spectacle of death so much and was leaving Edinburgh for a more civilised place. Bill didn't have the heart to tell him Dundee was the wrong town.

"They hanged our Margaret," Bill had heard him say with a gentle voice. Bill guessed he was a well-educated man. "Mad Maggie they called her, but she wasnae really mad. Simple, mind, not the full package, but nae mad. Anyway, since when is snapping an old woman's neck the way to solve our problems, eh? And the crowds. Oh my, they were chanting and screamin' for the hangman tae do his job. Nah, I'm getting oot before they hang an old man like me for nothing. I'm no watching as people laugh at my head being jolted back and the ketcher selling ma body to that crazy doctor for sticking his fingers in like a pie. Nae chance. I'm off."

Bill had overheard the tones of agreement from Mr and Mrs Cuthbert, and the passionate monologue was peppered with "oohs" and "aahs".

"Everything okay?" Bill asked over his shoulder as the sound of distant urination coupled with a deep sound of relief welcomed him from behind a tree.

The break hadn't come a moment to soon for Mr Cuthbert, Bill realised.

"Fine, thank you," the old gentlemen replied. "Fine."

"Could you please tell me how long to go, please, driver?" the younger man asked. Bill noticed that he kept glancing at an expensive watch on his left wrist.

"About 20 minutes, give or take," Bill replied as Mr Cuthbert came from behind the bushes, a smile forming on his slightly tubby, rosy cheeks as he straightened out his trousers.

"Better," he said and took his place in the carriage next to his wife, who was slightly more embarrassed than he was.

"As we're on a small break would anyone care for a little tobacco for the rest of the journey?" asked the smartly-dressed gentlemen with the dapper timepiece. He reached inside his overcoat pocket and brought out a small silver tin. "I have plenty to go around."

"Well, if you're sure," Mr Cuthbert said, looking to his wife for approval, "just what the doctor ordered, I believe."

"Oh aye," Bill replied, reaching out his hand. "Thanks kindly, mister."

"If you're sure? How pleasant and civilised," the old man said. Thoughts of the rope and the hanging of Mad Maggie now vanished from his mind.

The well-dressed gentlemen reached over, placing a pile of dry brown tobacco on a tissue and handing it to each of the gentlemen.

"And you, dear?" he asked the refined looking Mrs Cuthbert. "Go on," he urged, recognising the slightly mischievous glint in her eye. "I won't tell a soul, you know."

Mrs Cuthbert's face reddened as she looked at her husband. A slightly upturned smile formed on her full lips. "Oh go on, then," she said quietly. "A little tobacco never hurt anyone, *right?*"

"That's my darling," Mr Cuthbert beamed as the gentlemen leant over, the tobacco already in a fold of tissue.

Bill stood outside the open carriage door, his breath visible through the cold night. He gave Shadow another gentle stroke and removed the fine dry tobacco from the tissue, gently placing it on the back of his left hand. With a substantial sniff he breathed in its dry texture. As the moon shone down on the carriage, he was aware that his passengers were also enjoying the break. They were all inhaling the generous gift of tobacco, even the pretty lady. What could be better? They were in the countryside in the middle of the night, sharing a moment as they enjoyed one of life's luxuries. This thought, as well as the first class tobacco, mellowed Bill's mood even further. Life was beautiful. As he appreciated the wonderful scene around him, Bill noted that the well-mannered gentleman, the giver of such a fine gift, had yet to serve himself some of the delightful snuff. He hoped he hadn't been too generous and left none for himself.

As he stood staring up at the night sky, one hand stroking Shadow, the other facing downwards with the remains of the tobacco on it, he suddenly felt cold. His throat felt dry and exceptionally scratchy and his eyes became tight and itchy. He wanted to rip them out with his fingers, put them in a puddle of water, scrub them clean and place them back into his sockets.

What was happening to him? Thoughts of death and dying entered his fuzzy mind. Was this what it felt like? Why now? Was it the moon? The plague? His knees unlocked and his legs suddenly gave way, no longer able to support the weight of his body. Bill crashed to the ground as his throat continued to squeeze tight. His head began to throb, and it felt like a clamp was holding his head just above his eyes, pushing tighter and tighter. For all his doubt and inexperience in many things, Bill knew he was dying. He barely heard the piercing scream from Mrs Cuthbert or the crash of the elderly gentlemen as he tumbled from the carriage and landed on the ground below him. He barely heard the wheezing and coughing from the large mouth of Mr Cuthbert as he banged his large fist against the roof of the carriage. All these sounds came from a million miles away. He could hear only his blood thump around his head. His eyes remained closed and his throat continued to constrict.

As the sound of his own blood flooded his senses, Bill heard no more.

Some clouds went past the bright moon, temporarily sheltering the scene below it. They departed as Mr John Wilson stepped from the carriage, stumbling a little over the four dead bodies that lay in uncompromising positions around his feet. He gave Shadow a gentle stroke across the body, worrying for a moment who would look after him.

Horses are more intelligent than we give them credit for, he decided as he strolled confidently in the direction of Dundee. *Shadow will be just fine.*

CHAPTER VIII

PAUL MCKEANY SAT hunched over a table at the back of the Eagle Inn. Three times now he had nearly burnt his left ear on the candle attached to the back wall and three times a gaggle of ladies (if he could refer to them this way) had laughed in his general direction. His spectacles somehow dispersed the flickering light, giving him an imprecise awareness of the distance of the damn thing. He had completed his day's work and with pounds in his pocket had decided to pop to the pub for one of these new Indian pale ales he had heard so much about. But he was exhausted. There was no real reason for tiredness to take such a hold of him…it wasn't as if he was failing to get enough sleep, goddamn it. In fact, he got more sleep now than he ever did before he was married. Another sigh left his mouth and he took another large gulp of ale. Last night he had felt her body next to him. Although it was wrapped in far too much clothing than was necessary, he'd felt the warmth of her arm when it accidently flopped onto his side. As his stirrings began, he'd dared to make a move, shifting his arm slowly to her side, to her waist, to her….smack! The sting of pain in his hand was dull compared to the battering his pride had taken. And so it was. The stirrings lessened, his penis shrunk to its customary position and he was welcomed again to the world of sleep.

He ordered another beer and pondered upon the fact his work wasn't much more successful than his love life. He paid his money to the deformed barmaid and she slammed the drink on the table next to him. He didn't bother to even grunt a thank you and instead stared at the glint of the candle, ensuring he didn't get too near the flame. The frustrating thing was, he knew he understood the human body better than anyone. He'd grasped how the workings of the heart were somehow connected to the workings of the breathing system. He disregarded the miasma theory but had to hold on to that thought until he had more evidence. Of course it wasn't bad air that was causing disease. Why couldn't anybody else see that it must be something else? Something living. He thought the philosophy of phrenology was nonsense, too. Again, this was another scientific idea he knew he could disprove with a little time and effort. Was he the only one who realised the size of your nose or the angle of your forehead *didn't* influence your intelligence and how courageous or bold you were? But in order to show the world his revolutionary ideas he required specimens, specimens he could use to display his skill and his anatomical knowledge. He wanted to show off the human body in all its glory. But how on earth could he get such specimens? Where would one even start looking? *Maybe,* thought McKeany, *one would lead to the other.* He took another gulp of his ale.

"Anybody sitting there?"

McKeany's melancholy was disrupted by a large figure standing next to him. He was pointing to the empty chair. He recognised the man from Dundee city centre. He'd seen him around the local alehouses. Now he looked older somehow, as if he had a lot on his mind.

"Aye, go ahead," McKeany said, nudging the empty chair so the large man had more room to sit down. "Watch that candle. It's lethal. Tough day?"

The man removed his large hands from his pockets and stared at McKeany. His blue eyes were bloodshot and bags were almost visibly forming underneath his piercing stare.

"You could say that, mate. You could say that. You're that teacher, right? In the school up town?"

"Aye. I am indeed," Paul said, holding out his hand. "Doctor McKeany."

The larger man shook it back. "And I'm Geordie Mill," he said. "This place is a fucking dump, right?"

"Aye," McKeany agreed, removing his glasses and cleaning them on his sleeve. He decided to place them on the table rather than putting them back on his face. He felt intimidated and reckoned that losing the glasses might help him feel on even ground. But looking into Geordie Mill's eyes again made him realise he was wrong. He hoped his students wouldn't come into the tavern and see him talking to this coarse, savage man. It wouldn't do his reputation any good at all, especially if word got back to Charlotte's father. Nevertheless, McKeany appreciated the company. It was quite pleasant not to have to try and impress for a change.

"The good thing about this place is that it serves this stuff," he said, holding up his glass of ale. "At the moment it's very welcome, my friend."

"Aye," Geordie mumbled back. After a short pause he asked, "So, what's the problem? I mean, you must be fucking raking the money in with all these medical students. What a business you've got there, man."

"Ha, I wish."

"Really? I mean, look at me, man. No work on the docks, no work in the bars. You've got to fight and scrape for your living in this shitty fucking dump. At least you've got a trade."

"I suppose, Mr Mill," McKeany replied. He picked up his spectacles and placed them back down on the table. Maybe one day he would investigate why it was usual to start fidgeting when feeling intimidated.

"And fuck knows why, but people pay a lot of money to watch dead bodies being cut up," Geordie continued.

"Aye, Mr Mill," said McKeany, picking up his ale, "but first you need bodies. And believe you me, they cost an arm and a leg. I've got the money but I haven't got a clue how to get specimens."

The two men continued drinking their ales in silence. The taste of the beer soothed their minds as they considered their own issues. Finally, Geordie interrupted the quiet.

"Yeah, I can imagine. Christ, what are we like? Two grown men in a shitty ale house, one needing money and the other needing bodies."

Mill gulped the remainder of his ale down that large throat of his. "Oh well, better get on my way, I suppose."

Much to McKeany's dismay, he moved the candle and placed it in the centre of the table, inches away from his spectacles.

Even without them, McKeany noticed Mill's eyes darting around the place. He was like a rabbit aware that it was being hunted.

"Cheerio then, Mr Mill. I hope things improve."

"Aye, mate," Geordie said as he stood up. Then he immediately sat back down again. McKeany noted that his eyes had become two shades brighter. The blue was now overriding the red blood vessels, and he could also see the flickering light of the candle reflected in them. It reminded him how many view the eyes as the windows to the soul. The jury was out on whether Geordie actually possessed one.

Geordie smiled and it was one of the most devious, sinister grins McKeany had ever seen. He was glad he had left his spectacles off. More focus may have made his heart freeze. Remaining seated, Geordie Mill reached out his large hand again and McKeany, now slightly dumbfounded, shook it.

"Doctor McKeany," Geordie said, his voice steady. "I think this may have been a very productive evening. Very productive indeed. Now go and get us another drink. Let's talk business…"

PART TWO

CHAPTER I

Even though the temperature hadn't even reached 10 degrees, the street smelt of rotten fish and stale sweat.

Geordie stood still, grateful it wasn't the height of summer. The market stall had closed down for the evening but, as usual, fish carcasses lay sprawled along the ground. They attracted flies, which hovered around the decaying flesh. The sight made Geordie heave. *Absolutely disgusting*, he thought to himself, *it was no surprise that the place was smothered in rats*.

He had been to the same spot every day for the last 10 days in a row. During that time absolutely nothing had changed. *In fact,* Geordie mused, *it was depressing just how many people's lives involved the same mundane movements day in, day out*. Although in the case of the bank merchant, Peter Panwell, Geordie was glad of this.

The last few weeks had not gone to plan and he knew his current adventure could be the last throw of the dice for him. After that fateful meeting it had all sounded so easy, so transparently clear. Yet Geordie hadn't grasped the distances people would travel for fresh bodies. He was already acquainted with three body snatchers - one from London and two from Edinburgh. From time to time they came up to Dundee and managed to haul their delivery back again. This naturally made Geordie's job that bit more difficult. Retrieving a dead body from its burial place under the ground in Scotland carried a fine. Although a hefty fine, it could be worse. Stealing clothes from the deceased was what got you time in gaol. So Mill had decided to strip any corpses first and leave the clothes behind, an unpleasant job at best. However, the £10 price tag that scrawny teacher would pay would more than balance things out in the unfortunate event he was captured by the police or the Charlies. But Geordie hadn't foreseen how popular this current trade was. Things didn't help when a resurrectionist was interrogated in Cupar and informed the law he had been gravedigging in the Howff Cemetery for months and passing on bodies to a medical man in Glasgow. The Dundee Procurator Fiscal got involved and discovered there were at least four empty coffins in the ceme-tery. The Charlies were riled up, the police were riled up and now the public were riled up. *It was time*, Geordie thought, *to take a new approach*. And his plan was indeed a beauty.

Yet again he leant against the wall and watched the sad old woman enter the street five minutes after the last stallholder had packed up. He kept his beady eyes on her as she picked up scraps of vegetables and meat and placed them in her sack. Yet again he observed her scuttle around like a magpie before scurrying back through the lanes. Geordie had been observing this scene for 10 days, but for all he knew the woman may have been acting it out for the last 10 years. He looked again at his expensive watch. Well, expensive for some other sucker. He had found it and subscribed fully to the saying finders keepers. The fact that he found it on someone else's wrist didn't bother him at all. After six minutes he began to count the seconds. Three, two, one…and there he was, right on time again. Mr Peter Panwell was a very successful bank merchant and his suit and pocket-watch looked to Geordie to be worth more money than the whole of the East End. Geordie watched as he crossed the street, carefully skirting around any discarded scraps of fish. He looked at his pocketwatch one final time and walked up to his front door. Geordie hid in the shadows for the tenth time, watched the pocketwatch enter the banker's pocket for the tenth time and for the tenth and, hopefully, last time, heard the large sigh of relief that Mr Panwell expelled as he fished his keys out from his waistcoat, opened his front door and entered his abode, closing the door gently behind him again.

"Like clockwork," said Geordie quietly to himself as the upstairs light of the banker's house came on. He should have been saying it to his underlings, but since the night three weeks ago involving that spoilt rich brat and his unfortunate demise, Geordie had barely seen Jamie and Greg. They were still worried, of course, but Geordie had calmed their fears just enough to keep them on their toes. He didn't inform them about his encounter with Rosie. No fucking way was that cat being released from the bag. That information would have sent them over the edge, and if not the edge then to the new local force walking around town. No, he had kept them sweet, told them there was nothing to worry about while at the same time making it crystal clear that if he went down he would drag them kicking and screaming with him. Geordie realised they were more scared of being in the same gaol as him than they were about being caught. The thought made him smile and he'd managed to get them on board for a job that evening. He'd asked them to make sure they were at the safe house in order to welcome McKeany and make sure he had the money. He provided them with the address and a key. What he'd failed to mention was that they would have company: two friends of his from the Edinburgh side of Scotland. One of them was alright, but the other, well, even Geordie found him to be trouble. Anyway, at this moment in time, Geordie had to bear the brunt himself, so he continued to observe things from his position near the market stall. Geordie knew a man of habit when he saw one, and by god Mr Panwell was a man of tediously dull habit. He left work at 5pm, got to the tavern at 5.15pm and was back home by 9.30pm, six or seven drams later. Geordie knew the candle would flicker out in twenty minutes and if he listened carefully enough he'd hear drunken snoring kick in three or four minutes later.

"Like clockwork," he said again as he leant against the wall and awaited the inevitable. Again, Geordie's attention drifted to Rosie, that conniving, blackmailing, big-titted trollop. But even with thoughts of her sneakiness and nauseating attitude, he knew he was still attracted to the mad bitch. No, he must not get distracted with those lips, that enticing cleavage. *Focus, Mill, focus.*

He had scouted the area for days now, taking extreme caution and care as he observed the goings on behind the Nethergate, the new and popular destination that was home to the gentlemen's luncheon and dining rooms, plus a confection-ery establishment for the ladies. He was utterly sure the watch-men were paid up to the English Chapel only. No one gave them money to wander further up the street to the market, of that fact he was adamant. It was the gossip of the local drinking establishments that a dog had chased away someone robbing a flesher's shop around the corner. After closing up three hours later, some of the local market stallholders had found the thief still up a lamppost. That told Geordie these watchmen never went beyond where their ward would pay for. Why the fuck would they? It was indeed the talk of the pubs for many a night and it was the catalyst that gave Geordie the idea to monitor these out-of-zone areas. He knew that Panwell didn't have many friends, if any, and that he had a penchant for alcohol. He certainly had no family around him. And, of course, there was no dog. And until this damn Police Force found its footing, he was sure that no one would notice another man entering and leaving the building on a typical Thursday evening. Folk had other things to worry about, such as disease, poverty and these filthy gravediggers. The candle in Panwell's bedroom had been extinguished now for fifteen minutes. Geordie made sure the wheelbarrow he'd placed behind the candle stall's frame was still there. He took a deep breath as he caught sight of its handles through the haze, smiled his crooked grin and walked over to the closed front door of Panwell's living quarters. It was time to go and make a living.

*

Breaking into the house was the easy part, as was walking up the stairs. With all the alcohol in his system, Geordie was right to think Panwell wouldn't stir at the sound of a strong shoulder disengaging a cheap lock and a grown adult walking up to his bedroom. The test of his ability lay, however, in what he needed to do next. Geordie towered above the blanketed figure of the banker, who was producing snorting sounds as the air entered and left his nose. Geordie inhaled a deep breath himself and tried not to think about *what* he was about to do, but instead *why* he was about to do it. His mind focused on the price of this fine specimen. He could no longer be classed as a person. It was easier to think of him as a specimen ready for delivery. He couldn't afford to think humanly at a time like this. Instead he had to focus his mind and concentrate on the job at hand. If he succeeded, McKeany and Rosie would both benefit. In fact, maybe Panwell's customers at the bank would benefit, as they would no longer have to pay vast amounts of interest. Geordie felt his sweat drop down the crack of his backside as his knuckles tightened. He held a candlestick tightly in his right hand and was ready for action. Unaware, Peter Panwell continued to dream his final dream. Geordie hoped for his sake it was a pleasant one filled with women and booze. He raised the candlestick and held it steady. *Come on, Geordie,* he mused. *You have already killed one person. What's another one?*

In fact, it was that first bloody kill that had started off these shenanigans. *Fucking Jamie and Greg*, Geordie thought as he lifted the candlestick to eye level. *If you want a job done properly, do it your bloody self.*

He gently pulled the blanket up over the snoring face of Peter Panwell and, before he stirred awake, swung the candlestick twice at the lump where his head was. This was soon followed by the sound of a skull cracking and a final gargled choke. Geordie dropped the murder weapon and listened for the sound of breathing. There was none. He saw the blood sink through the blanket, took a deep breath and wiped his forehead, which was now sweating profusely. Then he began the not-so-pleasant business of dragging the banker's body downstairs and outside to his waiting wheelbarrow.

The times were a changin', and with cholera striking randomly and crime at an all-time high, Geordie knew people wouldn't bat an eye at the sight of a large man pushing a wheelbarrow through the streets of civilised Magdalan Green with a man-sized sack in it. Geordie pushed the wheelbarrow for half a mile, cursing both Jamie and Greg, whom he felt should be doing this donkey work. He continued to swear in their name, referring to them as a pair of "chicken shit useless bastards" as he turned the corner - the cobbled streets weren't making the wheel traction easy. *Oh well,* Geordie thought as he pushed his plunder around another corner. *The less money paid out, the more money for me.*

He smiled as he thought of the payment McKeany would give him for this. Maybe Rosie would change her tune. He might even take her to one of those Shakespeare plays the toffs had been talking about. The ones where men wore frilly costumes and talked funny. He would never understand the thoughts of the rich but if he was a part of their group he imagined he would fit in just right - even if that meant watching a load of shite. As he continued to push his wheelbarrow through the darkened streets of Dundee, Geordie found a whistle departing from his lips. Meanwhile, Peter Panwell remained as silent as a corpse.

CHAPTER II

THE CACOPHONY OF deafening sounds hit McKeany hard. He thought how one day he might get used to them, but not today. These parts of town would always fill him with anxiety and fear. The noise from carts' wheels and horses' hooves on cobbles clattered through his bones, as did the sound of traders shouting about their wares, beggars pleading and kids screaming. The hum of machinery from the surrounding mills provided a constant background noise. His hearing wasn't the only sense to be assaulted. His nose suffered from the offensive odour of the horse dung that caked the streets, cesspits filled with human waste, rotting fruit and vegetables and boiling whale blubber. With haste, McKeany continued his walk, which took him past a group of scavengers. They didn't seem to McKeany to be doing any waste clearance but were hunting on a different level and trying it on with the two hefty prostitutes over the road. They weren't in luck, it seemed. The women would almost certainly be hoping for gentlemen with full pockets, not these dirty young men with nothing but scraps of metal to offer. If McKeany was less nervous he might have admired their gall. The increase in factories shoving their smoke out into the air of late had done nothing to remove the area's other stenches and McKeany felt like he was on the constant verge of choking. At least now he had reached Broad Close and was just moments away from his destination.

The sight of an old door confirmed he had arrived where he was meant to be and he gave it a cautious knock, hoping Mill would answer and take the bag so he could be on his way again.

Instead, the door was opened by a gaunt youth who muttered a sentence in such a broad dialect that McKeany only heard the words 'Jamie and Geordie Mill'. He pointed to an uncomfortable wooden chair in between four other occupied ones. These were positioned around a table upon which were a pack of cards, some loose tobacco, piles of snuff and what appeared to McKeany to be a urine-filled jug. It was passed around the room as two of the men played cards and the other two sat watching.

What am I doing here? McKeany wondered as he took a seat. *This neglected house is full of debauchery.*

Plaster hung off the walls and the floor contained more mouse faecal matter than he had ever seen. Briefly looking around at the cast of characters he was surrounded by, he wondered if his discomfort was as plain to them as it was to him. If it was, they didn't seem to care. He declined when attempts were made to pass the jug to him and from then on in he was thankful that it consistently missed him. The last ten minutes had indeed been the longest of his life. The expression 'a fish out of water' didn't begin to describe McKeany's feelings as one of the card players slammed down his hand and shouted in a strong Edinburgh accent, "Gotcha, William, you bastard!"

"Alright, alright," said the other, passing over the coins to the louder one. McKeany felt a little more secure with the man who had just lost his hand. He seemed to have the respect of the others and his well-educated and gentle manner hinted he was a better and a more pleasant person that the others. His gentle, lilting Irish accent had a sing-song quality to it. Paul wondered how he'd ended up playing cards with such a ruffian.

"I thought you played this game in the army, Burke," said

the larger one, his voice booming through the small room, "you are truly shit at it."

"I'm just not concentrating really," said the smaller Irish gentleman. "I'm just thinking about Nelly and stuff. I'm looking forward to getting back west. You?"

"Aye," said the other, shuffling the pack.

*

McKeany recalled that Mill had called this a safe house, but to him this was anything but safe. The muscles in his backside tensed as he waited for the chair's flimsy legs to give way. He could always grab another chair, but he didn't want to draw any attention to himself. And besides, he figured that every piece of furniture in this house in Broad Close was as well-built as the one he was currently sitting on. This chair, this room and this part of the Overgate wasn't making McKeany feel comfortable at all. He scratched his neck as his eyes continued to dart around the room. He noted the lack of any pictures or portraits. The smell of stale sweat, mould and damp began to creep up his nose. He wasn't sure if it was coming from the sparsely-decorated room or its inhabitants. It was possibly both.

Not for the first time in the past minute he looked down at his bag. Mill had asked him to meet him here at midnight, with the money in a bag ready for his delivery. Altogether it came to six pounds and five shillings – the most money he had ever carried around with him. If the newly-formed Police Force had stopped him he would have been required to quickly think of some explanation for it. He had expected Mill to answer the door, show him the goods and take the money for future delivery. Then McKeany could go home to bed and that lovely yet very frigid wife of his. He should have known that life was rarely this simple.

McKeany noted how no one else in the room reacted to the two gentlemen playing cards. He'd been struck by the thinness of the man who had opened the door and invited him to sit. Now he was seated beside a young man who was as round as a barrel. They watched the card game and carried on passing around the urine-coloured liquid.

Three or four minutes later, the two card playing gentlemen scooped up their money and said to no one in particular, "Right, tell Geordie thanks, we'll see him around. We've got work to do in Edinburgh. A decent fucking town." Then they left the house.

Although McKeany was glad to see the back of the bigger fellow, it was now just him and the two younger guys. He heard them let out a sigh of relief as the door slammed shut.

Just as McKeany was about to find some courage and ask who they and the two card players were, they heard the sound of the front door being flung open, closely followed by the clatter of mettle. In walked Geordie Mill. He was dragging a sack through to the room. McKeany noted that the clatter was from the wheelbarrow, which had now been thrown down on its side.

"Alright, McKeany," he said, before clocking the two young gentlemen. "Oh, so you two bastards decided to show up, did you? I see. I do all the fucking hard work and you two just show up at the end and play happy fucking families. Is that how it fucking works now? Well, anyway, Mr McKeany, please meet Donald McGregor and James Jeffrey. Boys, this our new employer – he's a doctor."

McKeany slowly brought his hand out for them to shake and quickly retracted it as he realised they were still staring at the large, imposing figure.

"Eh, no, Geordie, you see…I thought, we thought, well we…we…felt bad so we thought we'd stay and, eh…help with the delivery…"

Greg's hat was firmly over his head as he stuttered, his eyes shielded to the world.

"Anyway, never mind you pair of useless fuckers," Geordie replied. Then he smiled as he asked, "Where did Hare and Burke get off to? Never fucking mind. I don't want to fucking know where those head cases got off to. Anyways, you're lucky I'm in a good mood."

The three men exchanged glances and the occasional subtle nod. Then Geordie broke the silence.

"Right, McKeany, you got the money?"

McKeany nodded and indicated to the bag next to his feet. In response, Geordie's smile filled the room. For a man who had just pushed a wheelbarrow containing a recently-deceased and fully-grown adult for the best part of two miles, he practically looked ecstatic. McKeany could smell Geordie's sweat, which was clinging to the air. The body odour of this half-crazed madman only added to his cloying presence.

They all looked down at the ground, at what appeared to be a sack of potatoes. Geordie had dragged in a very big, man-sized bag.

"Ladies and gentlemen, boys and girls," he laughed. "Welcome to our new service. McKeany, welcome to your doorway to fame and fortune, your ticket to the success you have been craving."

He opened up his arms like a conjurer and was obviously enjoying the theatre of his work. His overwhelming sense of pride was apparent to all and McKeany thought he was about to be sick. The odour emitting from Geordie's armpits didn't help matters.

Mill leant over and pulled open the sack, ready to empty its contents onto the ground. "I give you Peter Panwell, your first..."

As the covering came off, McKeany felt a slither of sick crawl over his tongue. The body thumped onto the ground then went still. Blood was caked over his face and the back of his head, and one of his arms was at an unnatural angle from the rest of his body. McKeany looked at the two younger men who appeared equally as pale.

"…specimen," Geordie continued.

It was then that the quiet groaning could be heard. McKeany was adamant it was coming from one of the two boys, but he daren't ask. He certainly didn't want these street criminals to think he was a posh, stuck-up lightweight with no backbone and an appetite for the morose, even though this description was, in fact, perfect.

The groaning gained a little volume and then developed into a full-on shout.

It was at that moment all hell broke loose.

All eyes were on the twisted, bleeding body of Peter Panwell. As he got to his feet with an almighty roar, one arm dangling from his side, the other holding his head, he resembled a wild beast escaping its cage.

"MY HEAD," he screamed, "WHY DOES MY BLOODY HEAD HURT SO MUCH?"

An almighty and seemingly endless roar followed.

As he watched this bloodied man rise from the floor, agony overtaking his body like a demonic spirit, McKeany began to scream. This was soon followed by the piercing screams of both James Jeffrey and Donald McGregor.

"Aaaaaaarghhh, he's come back from the dead. Aaaaargh"

Peter Panwell screamed with pain. Paul McKeany screamed with confusion. Jamie and Greg screamed with fear.

Geordie Mill realised he had to do something. With a few choice profanities he grabbed Panwell by the arm, pulled him out of the living room, past the wheelbarrow and out into the street, slamming the door firmly behind him.

A few seconds later, the screaming stopped.

"He'll be too disoriented to know what happened. And anyways, he never saw us," Geordie said when he came back inside. "He was blinded."

Geordie placed his hands on his knees and concentrated on getting his breath back. "And you three weren't any fucking help," he complained to his now crying partners in crime.

Wiping more sweat from his forehead, Geordie looked past the wheelbarrow and towards the closed front door.

"Shit," he said.

As McKeany already knew, some things were never, ever simple.

CHAPTER III

*T*HIS IS HELL'S *own back garden,* thought John Wilson as he
walked the cold streets of Dundee. *An absolute heap of scum.*
Scum built on scum built on scum. He was aware of its current
expansion from a small town to an industrial powerhouse, he
knew of its jute success and its linen manufacturing expansions.
He'd read about the shipbuilding trade and the city's pride in
having the largest whaling port in Europe. But he also knew
how this success was paid for - via the increased poverty and
shabby housing of the city's forsaken poor folk.

That's it, Mr Wilson thought as the toxic smell of whale
blubber invaded his nostrils, *that's their only saving grace.*

No wonder the Lord had sent him here. He *was* the foot
soldier, God's own private sergeant, the chosen warrior to begin
the cleansing process of the scum and dirt of this filthy shithole.
He had been here for no longer than ten days and already the
crime appalled him to the core. Two days earlier, just after he
had completed his new batch of special tobacco mixture, he had
read with revulsion that a pack of men had set their dogs on a
lone woman walking at the back of the Law. She had escaped
but her clothes were ripped to shreds. The next article described
how two warehouses, a heckle house and a locksmith had been
broken into as a result of robbers discovering how to cut keys.
He'd looked out the window of his temporary accommodation
and watched the rain falling on the pocket of Scotland where

God had given his trust to his people and they had repaid him by turning their town into an inferno of torment, pain and suffering. With a heavy heart he'd realised his planned stay of a month might have to be extended. The methodical approach of amalgamating arsenic and tobacco needed to be exact and the level of concentration it required left him exhausted. He wasn't getting any younger. But at least *now* it was complete.

He continued to walk through Seagate and onto Castle Street. In a nearby factory they were boiling blubber to make oil and the smell was overpowering. Wiping his face carefully with his hand, he straightened his bonnet and continued his stroll, beginning his work to cleanse Dundee of some of its troubles, which would hopefully bring him one step closer to the Kingdom of Heaven.

CHAPTER IV

THE LARGE WORKHOUSE dominated Hilltown. If the sun ever reached these parts it would cast a great shadow over the neighbouring street. Mr Joshua Cleaver stood up tall and rigid and admired his empire from the small section he referred to as his office. Everyone was working at top efficiency and this was good news all round. Mr Cleaver was more than aware that his employees worked hard, possibly harder than most. However, he was also aware that due to his foresight and forceful nature, many Dundonians had food on their table and were bringing up their children with the tools to succeed in this ever-changing world. Crime was high in the city and Mr Cleaver was a firm believer that hard work, a moral compass and a morning prayer provided the answer to this new problem. He encouraged his employees to attend church every Sunday. He was aware he could not *force* this, but he could *persuade*. Idle hands gave the Devil a job to do and by keeping the staff in his workhouse busy, there was simply no opportunity for that gremlin Lucifer to begin his mischief.

An old saying of his father's came to mind: *with power comes responsibility*. Occasionally matters didn't go quite to his liking. Being a good Christian man with good Christian beliefs, Mr Cleaver sincerely believed that every man, woman and child who had worked hard and attended prayer should be allowed into the Kingdom of Heaven. So, when the occasion arrived that some poor soul died in the workhouse, he sincerely hoped their family would come and collect the body, organise the burial and see the departed off. However, in the case of poor Nora Paul, Mr Cleaver was becoming slightly concerned. A quiet soul, she had passed away during her shift two days earlier. Her fellow workers had bowed their heads while her body had been moved into the back storage room, where it was cool and could remain until it was collected. Mr Cleaver was concerned that poor Ms Paul had no friends or family and the workhouse would have to organise the burial, which would not only cause expense, but set a precedent that he did not want to consider.

He was busy supervising his workers when a weight was lifted off his moral shoulders. A man and a woman clad in black came to the side door and asked to speak him.

The woman bowed her head, a veil covering most of her face. Mr Cleaver noted the sad shape her lips made, as if her life had gradually pulled the ends of them down towards her chin. The man was bulky and his black coat and sombre attire were fitting for this cold, dreary morning.

"This here," he said, placing his hand on the woman's arm, "is the deceased's sister. May we collect her? Is there a back door by which we may depart...for dignity's sake?"

"Of course, of course," said Mr Cleaver, showing the visitors in and walking them out to the chilly back store. He pointed to dear Nora Paul lying on a crate under a thin blanket of wool.

"Be still, dear," said the man. "Do not get too upset now. She will be in the Kingdom of Heaven to join your dear mother and father."

He crossed himself and looked to Mr Cleaver. "Thank you, kind sir, and God bless you. She...she loved working for you. She was privileged. Thank you. Is that the way out?"

Mr Cleaver nodded at the kind words. "Indeed," he said, "God bless her."

He waited until he'd reached his office before allowing himself to smile. Perhaps dear Nora Paul was no loner after all. She seemed close to her sister and brother-in-law. She would get a decent burial and, of course, the precedent was now yet to be set.

He looked over at his employees hard at work and thought no more about dear Nora Paul…

*

"I can't *believe* you, Geordie Mill. Since when did things change from me getting paid to suck on your prick to me lugging dead bodies down the fucking road for you? Anyway, how did you find out about….about *her?*"

Rosie nodded towards the weight they were holding.

"Have you heard the phrase 'the walls have ears'? Well, I play cards and go drinking with my walls and many ears. Anyway, shhhh, Rosie!" Geordie snapped as they carried the blanket-covered body of Nora Paul around the back of Hilltown and towards the shoe repairer's, where he hoped and prayed that useless pair, Jamie and Greg, would be waiting with the wheelbarrow. He'd naturally got the heavy, head end and his muscles were beginning to burn. This was a fact Rosie didn't give a shit about. She was still trying to figure out Geordie's walls and ears analogy.

"Anyway," Geordie said between gritted teeth. "This money's going to *you,* right? So once we're around this corner that's your part done. It's a small price to pay for such a quantity of money, I assume?"

"Are you sure this teacher fella will pay up? The way you've talked about him, he seems to me like a wet weekend."

"Of course he'll *fucking* pay up. Anyway, look, there are the boys. I can see them. Only another minute or two left."

"No need to swear. I mean, *you're* the one who managed to

fuck up your last job. Can't even strike a man properly, Geordie Mill. Your career in burking is just as successful as your skill in screw…"

"Shhhh," Geordie hissed as they placed the body on the ground next to the wheelbarrow. God, he was getting sick of this. It was difficult enough without Rosie consistently jabbing at him.

"Now, thank you for your help. But on you go now, dear, leave me and the boys to do the rest."

Rosie didn't need to be asked twice. She turned on her feet, threw off her veil, blew Geordie a kiss and walked off down the street. Geordie looked up at the thin, lanky figure of James Jeffrey standing next to the barrel-like Donald McGregor. He glanced back down at the dead body and then down the road to the tottering figure of Rosie. Geordie was beginning to curse the day he had met the big-bosomed, filthy whore. As she disappeared around the corner, he attempted to regain his composure. "Morning, lads," he said. "Right, make yourselves useful and pick her up, will you. Let's get her into the barrow before the world and his fucking wife sees what we're up to."

Jamie grabbed the head end and Greg took hold of the legs. Geordie was pleased to watch them squirm, as by now his face resembled a pig due to be slaughtered. He watched anxiously as the boys placed the body ungraciously into the wheelbarrow. Thankfully for all, it was still mainly covered with the grey blanket the workhouse had donated.

"Right, boys, we're going to McKeany's hoose. Place her…it…the package in his outhouse and we're done. Easy money where you can find it, right?"

He walked across Nethergate and the boys followed behind, pushing and steering the wheelbarrow through the cobbled streets of Couttie's Wynd. Although nearly 10.30am in the morning, no one looked twice at the trio. This was indeed the advantage of living in such a wonderful town. With the town's mayor bringing a trading boom, there were always areas that catered for society's less desirable folk. And this particular workhouse coincidentally happened to be right in the middle of such an area. Coutties Wynd joined up Nethergate and Yeaman's Shore, and no person would be walking these kind of streets for leisure. It was likely they were all up to no good too. Ironically, Coutties Wynd was named after William Couttie, a butcher. Geordie smiled at the coincidence. Although his confidence was indeed increasing, he wasn't out of the woods yet. He wouldn't be until the delivery was done and dusted.

Within twenty minutes *it* was done. McKeany had ensured Mill that his home would be unattended. His wife had arrangements elsewhere in the city and would be hobnobbing with others of her class. Meanwhile, McKeany was teaching. Geordie had picked up on the fact that not all was perfect in paradise for poor McKeany. He was glad that shit didn't only happen to the likes of him and his type. McKeany had, however, stuck to his word and left the key where he said he would. The boys managed to take the barrow down the side alley and deliver the package into the cold outhouse, leaving it covered on the ground. They locked the door behind them and left the wheelbarrow outside, propped up against the outhouse. This was a signal so McKeany would know that the job had been done. True to his word once again, he'd left the payment in the left corner of the outhouse, inside a small, used envelope. Geordie had counted the money as the boys had laid poor Nora on the ground. He'd smiled to himself as soon as he'd established it was the correct amount.

The three men left McKeany's and made their way to the high street. Geordie offered to buy them a drink. He knew, of course, that no one would decline the offer, but unbeknownst to them, he was paying for the drinks from *their* share of the takings.

CHAPTER V

THE PUBS AND alehouses didn't just serve alcohol. They were *not* just a place to play cards in, relax in and spend your hard-earned money in. They were *not* simply dens of sin where ladies of the night worked and looked for opportunities. They were *not* just disreputable areas of violence, gluttony, laziness and vulgarity. To people like Geordie Mill, they were sources of information, the sources of gossip. These tales of *who, where, why* and *how* were passed on to others to be judged by the men and woman who needed to justify their own lot in life. Or, as in Geordie's case, they could be used to meet his own needs. He saw them simply as his golden ticket to more opportunity.

He took a seat with Jamie and Greg at the same table where he'd fixed his partnership with Mr McKeany not two months earlier. It had been a bad start, even Mill would have owned up to that, but eventually he got the hang of things and to date had supplied five fresh bodies to the doctor. As he sipped on his ale, he mulled over how to retrieve the next ones.

Geordie's first victim, Mr Panwell, was still the manager of the bank, but he'd cut down on his nights down the pub. No one suspected that Geordie was involved in the attack and simply observed how Panwell seemed nicer these days, treating his customers with a little more respect and dignity.

"It's like he's met God and been told to be more pleasant,"

he remembered the old, one-toothed codger who frequented the Globe Tavern remarking once.

Geordie had smiled at that. Indeed, maybe he was Dundee's own knight in shining armour. He may go to heaven after all. To Geordie, though, finding out about a potential fresh body to track down was better news. When Greg got chatting to his neighbour, he made sure he paid attention. Although Geordie didn't know who he was, he looked like he'd seen better days. His skin was as ill-fitting as his clothes, his teeth resembled stones and his sparse hair clung to his head like loose thread.

"Any more bother with your brother's dog?" Greg asked him.

"Nah," answered the old man. "Nae bother. He's disappeared. Good riddance to bad rubbish, eh? He's probably sitting outside a butcher's shop in eternal hope. Fucking mutt. Anyways, did you hear aboot that poor Mary Hopkins woman. Poor mare."

"Mary, the nurse Mary?" Greg replied, taking a sip of his ale, "the one with the bairn."

"That's just it, Donald. The bairn has gone. Deed. Gave up the ghost and passed away. Gone to the great spirit in the sky."

Geordie rolled his eyes. If he hated anything more than people talking shite it was people using clichés. Greg had told him that the old man's wife had run off with a foreign dock-worker. Geordie was no way surprised if it was because she'd had to put up with that verbal shite all day long.

"Anyway, that's the problem, Donald. Not only is she looking for a lodger to fill that spare room of hers, but she's still got the body. The poor mare's had her bairn's body out in that spare room with no one ready tae pick it up. With that disease spreading, the undertakers are busy as hell. She's got to look at her baby's poor, pretty face all day long. Just thank the Lord it's cold in there."

Geordie's ears pricked up as he held his pint up to his lips. He continued to listen, only this time even more carefully.

"It's not as if that kid died with the pox or something," the old man continued. "She just stopped living. Poor Mary doesn't ken what to do with herself. Her dead daughter in her hoose and a spare room worth nothing because no one will rent it while there's a corpse in there. Poor cow. What is she to do?"

"Aye," Greg grunted before supping on his last mouthful of ale, "poor cow, alright."

And so it was. Opportunity had once again knocked on Geordie Mill's door and by hell he was ready and willing to answer it. Greg and his neighbour both looked up to talk to Geordie, but he had already left the tavern.

*

By the time he knocked on the door of 20 Shire Lane, Geordie had already washed his face and combed his hair the best he could with his grubby fingers. He flattened down his clothes so they weren't as rumpled as before and prepared to give Mary Hopkins the largest grin she had ever seen. He waited and knocked again. No answer. As the grin slid slowly south, he started to walk away. Then he heard footsteps and saw the door opening ever so slowly, by no more than an inch.

"Who is it?" Mary Hopkins asked in a timid voice.

Mill could tell she had recently been crying. The grin slid north again.

"Oh hello, Mrs Hopkins," Geordie said in his best gentle tone. To his own ears he sounded like McKeany. "My name is Mr Clarke and I've come to enquire about a room I heard for rent. I mean to stay for no more than a month at most and I am a most respectable gentlemen."

Geordie looked through the thin gap of the open door and saw a woman who would have been pretty if it wasn't for her swollen eyes and gaunt features. Geordie was prepared to bet she'd been a cracker in her heyday.

"I'm so sorry, Mr…"

"Clarke."

"Yes, sorry, Mr Clarke. But I'm afraid the room is unavailable. Have a good…"

Geordie's grin stretched a notch. "Please, Mrs Hopkins. "It is *only* a month at most and I won't need the room for, oh, I don't know, a few weeks. It's just that I find myself short of a place to stay."

He saw the look of hope in Mrs Hopkins' eyes. It was faint but present. She was thinking that a couple of weeks may be time for the undertaker to retrieve the body. He decided to try and close the sale before she had chance to change her mind.

"If I could simply look in the house itself. I do not need to see the room. Just the living quarters would be fine. Then of course we could come to some…arrangement."

Mrs Hopkins opened the door a little more. "I…I suppose that would do no harm," she said and opened the door fully to welcome in Geordie Mill.

"This, as you see, is the hallway and here on the left are the living quarters, where I spend most of my time of an evening knitting. Of course, you will be more than welcome to join me. "And this here," she added, pointing to a closed door, "is my room."

"Where would my quarters be, Mrs Hopkins?" Geordie asked, the smile now stuck firmly on that large face of his.

"Just to the left here," Mary Hopkins replied, pointing to the door, "but I'm afraid they are out of bounds just now. So sorry."

"Oh," said Geordie feigning disappointment, "have you already got a lodger?"

"Oh no, sir, nothing like that. You see…eh…eh…"

At that moment her courage crumpled and tears started flowing down her face. Geordie observed her shoulders rising up and down like a rag doll as a wail departed from her small mouth. He stood still for a minute or two and then, as gently as possible, touched her right arm.

"Whatever is the matter, dear?"

"Oh, Mr Clarke, you will neither want the room or anything to do with me after this," she continued, snot forming beneath her small nostrils. "But I cannot hold the pretence any longer. You see, my dear daughter passed away not last week and the undertakers are yet to come. My little darling sleeps quietly in that room."

With that, another flow of tears broke through the mother's saddened eyes.

Geordie Mill waited for the hysterics to subside. Then he very gently took her arms and, bowing his head softly, said, "Hush hush, dear Mrs Hopkins. What a *poor* wretched situation you are in. Poor, poor girl."

He tucked her face gently into his chest for comfort and support, hoping that in her grief she wouldn't notice the stench of smoke and alcohol.

The sobs subsided and her tears carried on flowing. "Oh, Mr Clarke. You are such a gentle, caring man. I am so...so...sorry that..."

"Hush, my dear," he replied softly, letting her weep some more. If supplying bodies didn't earn him the money he needed, Geordie considered how he might get a job as one of them actor fellows. He was, as he was ready to admit, very good at it.

"Hush now, Mrs Hopkins. You have indeed been through the hardest of times, you poor creature you. May I ask a favour, though? I don't know if I said previously but for many years now I have been involved in the clergy. And well, I like to think I have a, shall we say, understanding of God and his disciplines. May I...and if it is too much trouble, please decline...look at the little innocent?"

Mrs Hopkins looked up at Geordie Mill and wiped the last tear from her eye.

"Could you, I mean would you, bless her?"

Hope and salvation, thought Geordie. Everyone wished for such. "Of course, dear. I can indeed if you would like."

And with that Mrs Hopkins led Geordie into the sleeping quarters. The windows were wide open and the room was ice cold. The body of a six or seven-year-old child was positioned under a sheet.

Mrs Clarke began to sob again. "I hate leaving her here, you understand, but until the undertakers can take her with the promise of a suitable burial, God rest her soul, what am I to do?"

Geordie gently leant over, pulled down the cover and looked at the pale ghost of a girl. Then he gently placed the sheet over her face and calmly walked over to the open window, his inner actor carrying out a look of pensive wonder as he pretended to reflect on the glories of Heaven. In reality, he was calculating dimensions, angles and escape routes. He soon put thoughts of his wheelbarrow to one side and said out loud. "We must all come to this sooner or later."

He slowly walked past the occupied bed and back towards Mrs Hopkins, leading her by the arm out of the hallway and into the living quarters. He motioned for her to sit down, then placed her hands on her knees and covered them with his own.

"Mrs Hopkins, you have been the victim of pure bad luck. I am sure the undertakers will remove your darling daughter and she will get the burial you so desire. In the interim, I will take the room as soon as it is vacated."

"Oh my, oh my, Mr Clarke. How can I possibly thank you?" she said, tears flowing from her pale face once more. She looked to Geordie like a woman who had slowly and gradually had the worries of the world placed on her shoulders and then removed with one swoop. Her grief had turned to a kind of joy. She was half smiling, half crying.

"I suppose we should talk about finances, Mrs Hopkins,"

Geordie said, "but first let me get us a stiff drink to solidify the offer and toast future success."

He stood up and removed a bottle of whisky from his inside pocket. Then he went into the kitchen and helped himself to two small cups. It was easy to navigate and Ms Hopkins didn't seem to mind the intrusion.

Geordie supposed that once a knight in shining armour has lifted a great weight off your shoulders, then helping yourself to two small drinking containers can be forgiven. He placed a little whisky in each cup and sat himself down on the seat next to Mrs Hopkins, who was still half smiling at the dual thought of a decent burial for her poor daughter and her future financial prospects thanks to a well-suited gentleman lodger.

"Bottoms up," said Geordie, lifting up one of the glasses and placing the other in Mrs Hopkins' hand.

"Pardon?"

Damn it, thought Geordie. The mask had nearly slipped. Confidence sometimes did that to a man. Thankfully he regained his composure and looked her in the eye.

"Oh, I heard that is what they say in the local taverns, Mrs Hopkins."

"Oh," she replied. "Those places are such disgusting buildings. Places of sin indeed. They should be knocked down and churches replace them. That's what would make this country great again."

"I utterly agree with you, Mrs Hopkins. Absolutely filthy they are. They harbour crime and god knows what else."

He was disappointed that the cup remained stationary in her hand.

"The Book of Proverbs states that 'the Lord looks down upon those that have lying tongues, shed blood and run into mischief'" Mrs Hopkins quoted.

"I would say, Mr Clarke, that these dens of sin contain all these people, would you not?"

"Absolutely, Mrs Hopkins," Geordie agreed, staring at the cup, which still hadn't got any closer to her lips. "I couldn't agree more. Anyway, let us drink and conclude this fortunate turn of events."

He brought his own cup to his lips, but made sure they remained closed. Then he watched as Mrs Hopkins took a small sip, blinked at the strong taste and then emptied her cup. Soon after she closed her eyes, a slight smile forming on her lips.

*

Mrs Amy Hopkins awoke four hours later. She noted the glass on the table and felt a slight feeling of hunger. She recalled her meeting with Mr Clarke and his understanding and patient tones. He was a typical man of God and the church. She wondered when he had let himself out. Guilt formed a little as she thought of her poor manners. Falling asleep whilst conversing was indeed poor etiquette, however, she was sure he would forgive her for that. He was a man of the cloth after all. She hoped he had left a note with the time or day he would be returning or bringing the deposit. Had she mentioned the deposit? Come to think about it, had they talked about the cost of the room at all? Her head felt fuzzy, but she managed to stand up nonetheless. She rubbed her face with her fingers and went to check on her beautiful girl. Every evening she went in to wish her good night and promise her a swift burial so she could play with the angels.

As she went into the room, the first thing she noticed was the empty bed. Then she began to really cry.

CHAPTER VI

WHYTE AND BOYD sat at the kitchen table facing the red, bloated face of George Law. They were representing the new Dundee Police Force and fidgeting within their new authoritarian attire. Graham knew he was angry and understood to a certain degree why, but for God's sake couldn't he calm down and see a bit of reason?

Common sense wasn't so common, and when panic prevailed in a city, reason hid well out of the way. *Panic*, reckoned Graham Whyte, *travelled quicker than the plague, especially in growing cities such as this one.*

Law's wife was standing behind him as he ranted, barely taking a breath.

"So *what* are you doing to find these body snatchers? He's lucky to be alive, you know. *Lucky.* And you two sit here and want to question him. Hasn't the poor bugger been through *enough?*

As he talked his jowls seemed to move separately from his mouth. His wife, who was as thin as a rake, tutted and shook her head, her arms crossed over her lean body as she agreed with every word her husband uttered. Craig wondered if she *ate* anything at all. If not he had no doubt where the food went to.

"You see, Mr Law," Craig interrupted, "it's not that we don't believe your son. It's just we *have* to be sure. And you know, get a description of the gentlemen."

"He gave us one, he said they were dressed smartly," Mrs Law said sharply. "Why must he talk to you guys? You'll scare him half to death. Don't you think he's been through enough?"

This is getting nowhere, mused Craig. But it was no surprise. Over the last few months he had witnessed fear and panic take over Dundee, from the Ferry to the West Port. As the Police Force grew, unfortunately so did the misdemeanours. The rise of burkers and gravediggers was a blight on society, and it simply had to be stopped. Chaos was occurring and there seemed no cure for it. Only two weeks earlier, a child's body had been stolen from the burial ground at the Howff. Although 10 guineas had been offered as a reward, no arrests had been made yet. To Craig Boyd and Graham Whyte, this was no surprise. They knew the bodies were being transported to Edinburgh and even further afield, and the going rate was up to 20 guineas.

People were angry and scared. It was a bad combination. And now Boyd and Whyte sat in the Baltic Street home of George Law, the shoemaker, investigating another possible burking attempt.

As the story went, Mrs Law had answered the door to her nine-year-old son, who was in such a state of panic he could barely move. The smell of alcohol followed him in the house. Mrs Law immediately called the doctor who was of the opinion that the young boy was drunk. By the time Mr Law reached home, their son started complaining of a sore head. Another doctor was called and it was then the boy revealed what had happened. Two smartly dressed gentlemen had forced him to drink something from a bottle and then tried to drag him to the Meadows. The boy had objected with all his might, managed to break free and run all the way to his front door.

"It's plain to see, gentlemen, that these two men were bodysnatchers and are now selling children's bodies to the anatomists. *Children's bodies*, I tell you! It's disgusting, it's putrid and *you* have to catch them. I mean, the damn Charlies are fuck all good!"

George Law's face was reddening further as his knuckles got whiter.

It's only a matter of time, thought Craig, *until that large fist goes through the table.* He noticed that Mrs Law had a concerned look on her face. He had the impression she had witnessed Mr Law lose it this way before.

"I understand, sir. If we could just speak with your son for a min..."

At that moment, the door squeaked open and in walked a dirty-faced nine-year old. His dark eyes appeared troubled and tearstains were still apparent on his grubby cheeks. His short, spiky hair carried a leaf. He'd obviously been standing outside and he looked first at Whyte and Boyd before going to stand next to his mother.

"So," Craig said gently. "Those two gentlemen. How were they dressed?

"Eh?" the boy's eyes widened and he looked at his mum and dad. His mum nodded slowly.

"Eh, they were, eh...both scruffy looking like..."

"Scruffy? I thought you said they were well dressed, son," said Law, his voice booming despite his attempts to quieten it.

The boy looked more scared than before. "Eh, yeah...they...they were smart. That's what I said."

The boy noticeably shivered as four pairs of eyes looked down at him. His own eyes dropped to the floor and tears started rolling down his cheeks as if in a race to the floor. Snot formed at the entrance of his nostrils. He started talking and it reminded Boyd of a damn bursting.

"They were well...no, yeah kind of...I'm sorry, there were *no* men. I made...I made...I made it up. Me and Skody found a square bottle. We knew we shouldn't have drunk it, but we did and we thought you would tell dad...and...and he would tell me off. I ne...I...ne...ne...never wanted to get anyone in trouble."

The Laws looked at their son who had just admitted his crime. It was no biggie really. Both his parents turned to Whyte and Boyd.

"Sorry for wasting your time, gentlemen," said George Law, standing up to show the policeman the door. His jowls continued to wobble, but slower this time.

"Don't be too hard on him," Graham said, "we've all been young once, right?"

"Right," Law replied. He didn't look convinced.

As Craig Boyd and Graham Whyte stood outside the closed door of the shoemaker's house in Baltic Street, they burst out laughing. Bad times or not, kids were always going to be kids. But, as they both knew, there was a serious side to this confession. Panic and fear was undoubtedly squeezing into every pore of the city, and something was soon set to burst.

CHAPTER VII

GEORDIE MILL SAT on a wooden chair directly opposite the drunken undertaker and stared at him squarely in the eyes. James Jeffrey sat to his left, shuffling his chair ever so slightly and attempting to master his intimating look, which he was failing woefully at. Thankfully, Geordie Mill was an expert in such matters. He kept his eyes on the grey-haired old undertaker who was finding it difficult to peel his sad, bloodshot eyes away from the expensive bottle of whiskey Geordie clutched tightly in his hands. Geordie kept up his stare, glaring into the already beaten eyes of the old man.

Maybe this is what happens when you spend your day with corpses, Jamie thought. *When the main company of your day are the dead bodies of men, women and children.*

He also wondered if this poor man had a wife or any friends. He doubted it somehow.

Geordie continued to talk, his stare constant.

"Are you sure you don't want to make a deal, Mr Edwards? I mean, would anybody ever find out?"

Mr Edwards' eyes remained fixed on the bottle of whisky. Jamie noticed that Geordie was holding it so the label was exposed.

"I-I-I suppose not. But…but…but my re…re…re…"

"Reputation?" Geordie boomed, his large, bulking figure spilling over the edge of the narrow seat. "Reputation? Really,

Mr Edwards. As I said, no one would ever find out. Unless of course you blabbed."

"No-no, M-M-Mr Mill, of course I-I-I wouldn't."

Jamie actually felt sorry for the old fellow. Geordie Mill had him by the short and curlies, and he bloody well knew it. Jamie knew from experience that Geordie had a knack of getting his own way.

Take tonight, for instance, he should be enjoying a dram or two with Greg in the Tavern or trying to get somewhere with the Carol girl he'd taken a fancy to. But no, here he was helping to persuade an ageing, alcoholic undertaker to give them some of his dead bodies. Jamie wondered where it had all gone wrong. His mother would be so disappointed.

"And think of it, Mr Edwards. All the work you do looking after these beautiful souls until they join their loved ones in the earth. And what do you get for it? I bet you the families don't even pay you enough for a decent drink, do they?"

"They...they can't afford to, Mr Mill. That's why they c-c-c-c-come to me. I'm cheap, Mr Mill, I do it for respect not financial gain."

Geordie shuffled in his chair, moving slightly forwards and leaving only inches between their faces. His smile reminded Jamie of a wild dog in preparation for a meat feast.

"Absolutely, Mr Edwards, you are fully respected," Geordie said, his smile getting wider, his teeth glowing in the dull, small space that was the undertaker's office. "And they will still give you the respect you deserve. They will still bury their dead, Mr Edwards. I mean, not actually their dead, but it's the thought that counts, Mr Edwards, isn't it. The emotional aspect. Surely it doesn't matter if the actual body is present, as long as they think it is. Just imagine finishing off a day of cleaning, wiping and scrubbing these dead bodies, God rest their souls, with a small dram of this..."

Geordie made the sign of the cross then shook the bottle for effect.

Jamie swore he could see a sliver of dribble leaving Mr Edwards' thin lips as his old eyes widened. But Geordie wasn't quite finished.

"But, Mr Edwards, this is only one bottle. There are plenty more where this came from. Let us say a bottle for what, five bodies? Oh, what the hell, four bodies, Mr Edwards. A bottle of whiskey for four, healthy young bodies. I'll be giving it away next."

Geordie's eyes never left Mr Edwards as he popped off the top of the whisky bottle and took a slug of its contents. Jamie could see the old man's throat contracting, as if he was trying to swallow his desire for just a wee taste of what Geordie had.

"But…but what will ha…ha…happen if someone notices the coffin is too light, Mr Mill?"

Geordie's smile remained in place. "I'm sure you could figure out that one, Mr Edwards. I mean, I'm sure a healthy body could be replaced by potatoes, a disease-ridden kid by a bunch of rags. I'm sure you could do the maths."

Mr Edwards winced and Jamie realised Geordie had taken this too far. He had pushed his luck and the deal was off. In a way, Jamie was pleased. Maybe there was a God looking down at them after all.

Geordie kept his gaze and took another swig from the bottle.

"Of course, this bottle has had two mouthfuls taken from it, Mr Edwards. So this one is only worth two of your bodies." He followed this statement with one of the most sinister grins Jamie had ever seen.

Jamie realised that Geordie had gained back control. God must have been distracted.

Mr Edwards stood up slowly and took a deep breath. His patchy grey hair flopped over his gaunt face and Jamie noticed just how brittle he was. He took another look at the bottle of whisky in Geordie's hands and then glanced behind him, where two large, wooden coffins lay on the ground, one noticeably larger than the other.

His eyes flicked to the other corner of the room where a pile of rags and a sack of grain had been placed. Jamie realised food wasn't a priority for Mr Edwards. His life was surrounded by dead people and alcohol, and the first necessitated the second.

"Okay," Mr Edwards said, his whole body reflecting the nature of his defeat. "Deal."

Geordie passed the bottle to Mr Edwards and got up from the wooden chair, Jamie following suit.

Mr Edwards clutched the bottle tightly, as if he half suspected Geordie to take it back off him.

"So, same time next week? And a new bottle?"

"Absolutely," said Geordie cheerily as he walked over to the two coffins. "Now, give us a hand, Jamie. I mean, that's why I invited you. These bodies won't walk out of here on their own."

As Geordie laughed and Mr Edwards took a long-awaited sip of the spirit, Jamie felt a little sick.

CHAPTER VIII

"**E**XCUSE ME, LADIES," Paul McKeany said timidly as he walked into his living room. Charlotte and her cousin Betsy stopped talking and looked down at their knees, waiting for him to leave. McKeany found the black umbrella he'd been looking for and shuffled towards the door. As he opened it, he heard Charlotte let out an audible sigh. "I'm so sorry, Betsy," he heard her say. "I thought he would never leave."

The remark was followed by a childish giggle. McKeany let go of the handle, straightened up his jacket, looked into the hallway mirror and took a deep breath, attempting to bring his chin up high. When Charlotte's cousin Elizabeth, or Betsy as her girlfriends called her, was staying over, things were worse than ever at home. It was difficult enough being ignored all day and every day by your own wife, but when Betsy was around, Charlotte made constant jokes at his expense. Over the past few days he'd overheard words such as 'worm', 'wet', 'tiddler', not to mention the expression "all brain no trousers". He heard Betsy remark how unlucky Charlotte was for picking a duffer.

"He's no sailor, that's for sure," she'd said. It made McKeany feel like he was an imposter in his own house. Quite frankly, he'd had enough. And to top it off, if humiliation and anger weren't enough, things in the bedroom were also declining (if that was at all possible). However, professionally it finally looked like he was getting somewhere. Money was short and the risks were getting greater, but soon he would have all the ingredients he required to succeed in his venture.

Knox, eat your heart out, he thought as he left the house and walked into the back garden, where his small outhouse stood. Removing his keys gently from his pocket, he unlocked the door, lit a lantern and shut himself inside. The outhouse was small and designed to store outdoor tools. Not that he was a man for gardening. McKeany had never been much for labouring. He liked to think that his brain was his major muscle, the workhouse for his body. He took a deep breath and slowly moved the plank of wood that had been propped up against one wall. He now had access to a large pile of rags that the plank had been hiding. He took another deep breath, gulped in as much fresh air as he could and removed the top rag from its position. Through the dim light he could see a bare, pale arm hanging limply. He recognised it belonged to a juvenile and knew without looking what lay beneath it...six more of the deceased...six more dead souls that should have been resting in peace. Instead, they were lying here in a large pile in his outhouse. Stuffed onto a pile like wood for a bonfire, they'd been afforded no dignity, no respect.

McKeany's breath hung in the air as he looked at the young female arm again. Here he was, a teacher with a beautiful wife and a large house, collecting dead humans like a ratcatcher collected vermin. He looked at the arm again and thought of the newly-formed Dundee Police Force. What if they somehow discovered the bodies? He imagined Charlotte and her damned father tutting as he was led away in handcuffs. Had he gone too far? Maybe he should pay Geordie to recollect the bodies and dump them in the Tay. Maybe he should forget this whole project whilst he still had some dignity left. He stood still, his breath hovering in the cold air, his workhouse brain working overtime.

Who was he kidding? Dignity? He looked through the

outhouse's tiny window towards the main house. He imagined Charlotte and Betsy giggling over the size of his manhood, comparing him to Dundee's dockworkers and sailors. Where the hell was his dignity?

He looked up at the pile of bodies and imagined one of them on a clean, sparkling table. Next to it an assistant was waiting to pass him his surgical implements. He saw himself taking to the floor, pacing up and down in front of the naked specimen. His large audience would gasp as he made the first incision and proceeded to demonstrate his knowledge of the heart, lungs and kidney. He'd show these young minds how these systems worked in synchronicity, despite what Dr Knox said in his lectures. They would pay handsomely for such experiences and he would be the toast of Dundee, Edinburgh and London and revolutionise the knowledge of the human body. McKeany gently pulled the blanket over the cold arm and replaced the plank of wood. As he locked the door of the outhouse, he pushed his glasses up his nose and then walked back towards the house, where the two women would continue their gossiping oblivious to the potential of the man who had just re-entered the building.

CHAPTER IX

M R WILSON PLACED his cup back in its saucer, cherishing the tea's aftertaste. It was a delightful brew indeed. He was visiting his new friend, Thomas Abbott, whom he'd met while out looking for lodgings. They found themselves stopping for a rest on the same bench and struck up a conversation.

Fate, Mr Wilson mused, *is often an unfortunate affair.*

Abbott was a very nice if dim-witted man, but Mr Wilson found him to be pleasant enough company nonetheless.

Unfortunately, he had been sacked from his job on the docks for falling asleep while on a night shift. Although not the biggest crime in the land, this happened to occur at the same time as a gang of copper stealers were lumbering around. They'd walked over his sleeping body as they hauled away their loot. This did not bode well for Abbott and the foreman got rid. Since then he'd be looking for employment but was held back by his melancholy nature and slow speech.

It was now his fourth visit to Mr Abbott's house and Mr Wilson took the opportunity to offer him some snuff. The tobacco was of good quality and Thomas Abbott happily accepted the gift.

In his defence, Mr Wilson did not enjoy seeing a friend choke on his own vomit whilst trying to scrape out his own eyeballs, but cyanide did have that effect on people, friend or not. Once Thomas Abbott stopped garbling and proceeded to choke on his own tongue, Mr Wilson put on his jacket and left the man's home, closing the door firmly behind him. Some jobs were more difficult than others, but Mr Wilson knew that God worked in mysterious ways.

*

"This is shite, Boydy and you know it."

"Aye," replied Graham Whyte. "It is indeed."

Craig Boyd and Graham Whyte sat on the foot-high wall behind the William Adam Town House. Three months ago the building had given both men inspiration and hope. Now the large construction, which amongst other things housed the jail, filled them solely with despair.

Their beat today was to walk the path of the meandering Dens Road and the steep slope of Bonnethill, where factories, tenements and mills had been born. The mere thought of their forthcoming six-hour stint left them drained. The life had been sucked out of the once gregarious men. It had been a difficult couple of months and they both knew that things could well get worse. In fact, they would get worse. Crime had always been rife, but they had mostly been opportunistic ones. Now teenage gangs roamed the city streets freely. Only the week before, a nine-strong gang of kids ran away with copper stripped off the brig of the *Commodore Napier*. Of course, heads were rolling and the superintendent was sparing no one from the full force of his wrath. His lieutenant, office keeper, turnkey and six sergeants, Whyte and Boyd included, received his royal reprimand that morning. Counting the 36 watchmen, Dundee had a total of 46 men involved in trying to keep the peace. It was hardly enough to keep control of a city in ruins. With the increasing number of suicides, the three reported deaths from arsenic poisoning, the street gangs, an increase in crimes of passion and, above all, the endemic of bodies being dug up for this new wave of medical science, Dundee was a city going to hell in a handbasket. During his half-hour long tirade, the superintendent also mentioned how in Calton, Glasgow, not a million miles away, the police force had been issued with cutlasses. When one officer hacked the arm off a resurrectionist, the criminal in question requested to keep it to sell on to a medical student.

Also in Calton, a drunken man turned up at the funeral party of his nephew demanding that his body be sold to anatomists.

The message was that with its thriving jute and whaling industry, Dundee was soon going to be a den of crime too. *Soon? Hell, it was a den of crime.* And it was their job to expose this den and stop the rot, no matter what the personal cost. To make matters worse, the general public were beginning to vent their frustration over the rising crime levels on the police force. A young officer called Edward Monahue had been walking his beat at Seagate when someone set his mastiff on him. Two days before that, a James Wilson from Coupar Angus Road attacked two lieutenants as they dealt with an incident in which a cloth manufacturer had bitten a watchman's hand in retaliation for a body being stolen. The meeting had concluded with the promise of better equipment for both the police and the watchmen, including waterproof hats and shorter, less cumbersome coats.

"Suppose we better get going, Whytey," Craig Boyd said.

"Aye, right you are."

The men reluctantly stepped off the wall and began their shift, their boots scraping against the dirty cobbled streets.

CHAPTER X

PAUL MCKEANY WATCHED Dr Jacob MaCraig-Robinson's thickset, grey eyebrows form a V shape over his sunken blue eyes. It amazed him how you could literally see the old man thinking. He'd dealt with him many times before, so McKeany knew what to expect and wasn't disappointed when MaCraig-Robinson's fingers locked together and his eyebrows sharpened into a final V formation, resembling seagulls readying to land. He exhaled deeply through his nose, causing his nostril hairs to slowly waft in the exiting breeze.

"So, McKeany, you're sure you want to begin the anatomy course *here* in *Dundee?*" he asked. This was the fourth time he'd asked the question and McKeany knew he was posing it more to himself. McKeany nodded once again.

"It is true, Mr McKeany, that the Corporation of Surgeons in both Edinburgh and London have stated that the study of medicine and surgery is much hampered by the scarcity of opportunities by which the students might get a practical acquaintance with the anatomy of the human body. It is *also* true, Mr McKeany, that we need more young anatomists up here in the North East. Our students are indeed spending their hard-earned money or, should I say, their father's hard-earned money, on the sights of the south. As you very well know, in my opinion, the damn south needs no more advantages with this."

McKeany nodded at this statement. Of course he agreed with it. After all, he'd brought it up as soon as their meeting began.

"And of course, these students, who we would *deeply* love to have up here in the North East would be properly taught in the practicalities of anatomy?"

"Of course, sir."

"You see, our good friends at the Corporation of Surgeons have now insisted, as is their want, that in order to produce a certificate of anatomy, one must attend at least two courses of dissection. After all, we want the students to leave these lessons as *surgeons* not *butchers*. I'm sure you agree to that, Mr McKeany?"

McKeany continued to sit up straight, his chin up, his spectacles firmly resting on his thin nose.

"Absolutely, Doctor," he replied. "We need our students to become experts in their field. So they in turn can teach *their* students, and so on. This knowledge about man is just beginning, Dr MaCraig-Robinson, we are pioneers in the field and we must take some responsibility in the future development of medicine by giving these students the drive to begin this epic journey into the world of both science and God!"

The words rolled off his tongue just as he had planned. Last night, while his beloved Charlotte was wrapped in her many layers of nightwear, McKeany had gone downstairs to the living area and practised his speech 10 or 15 times in front of the mirror. As he watched Dr MaCraig-Robinson unlock his fingers he noted the grey-haired seagull lift its wings. He knew then that all the practice had been worth it. Anyway, it wasn't as if he'd been missing out on any lovemaking. He could only hope his success would trigger that particular desire of his into action.

"But have we got that many specimens, Mr McKeany? I mean, I've heard stories, my dear chap, of bodies costing up to 16 guineas, which is, of course, more money than the students would pay. I understand that you are an honest man, Mr

McKeany, but in these awful times, so-called resurrection men are offering schools like ours bodies to dissect. I mean, why *would* we support such a crime? The law can be an ass sometimes, as we are all aware. And as *you* are aware, Mr McKeany, only the bodies of murderers or those who have given direct permission can be used for this practice. How can you be so sure this will be the case here?"

Paul McKeany smiled and pushed his glasses further up his nose. His acting was getting as good as Mill's. Mr Shakespeare could eat his heart out.

"Oh dear, oh dear, I never even considered that," he said looking as shocked as he possibly could. "Of course, sir, as I already stated, my brother is the turnkey of the newly-appointed Police Force. You would be *amazed,* sir, just amazed at how many of our criminals fail to survive the jailhouse. In fact, we would be doing *them* a favour. And indeed, they need all the help they can get."

"They do indeed, they do indeed," said Dr MaCraig-Robinson, vigorously nodding his head and giving the seagull a hesitant flight. "Well, Mr McKeany," he continued. "We will discuss the logistics sooner or later, but congratulations, you are now officially Dundee's first anatomical lecturer. Now, dear boy, maybe you can get on to that brother of yours. Get some specimens delivered to us, eh?"

Paul McKeany stood up and shook Dr MaCraig-Robinson's hand. "Of course," he grinned.

He left the room with a spring in his step. Thoughts of the body count reducing in his outhouse, gasps from the hundreds of students watching him display his masterly experience in the theatre and lovemaking with dear Charlotte filled his thoughts on the carriage journey back home. It was a very pleasant ride indeed.

CHAPTER XI

GEORDIE TURNED ON his side and attempted for the fifth time in 20 minutes to get a feel of Rosie's prize assets. And for the fifth time in 20 minutes, she flicked his hand aside as if she was squatting away an annoying fly. He exhaled deeply and audibly through his nostrils and crossed his arms tightly across his chest. Damn it, he had missed a game of poker for this shit.

Tonight had been a total nightmare. In fact, it had probably been one of the worst fucking nights of his entire life. Instead of plotting, scheming or working, Geordie had decided to head down to the Eagle Inn to sink back many drinks and win some money against Reverend Smith and his cronies. His pockets were full and by the end of the evening he expected his belly and his pockets to be even fuller. But no, tonight life had promised him peaches and brought him a rotting fucking apple core instead. He saw her just as he was leaving his home. Rosie Trayling, his one-time bit on the side, presently now the demon on his fucking back. She was obviously waiting for him, standing bold as brass with one foot cocked on the wall behind her, her bosom pushed tightly into her top.

"Hi there, big boy," she said. "You looking for me?"

"Well, it's good to see you, Mr Mill," she continued before Geordie could reply. "Come over here, big boy. What did I hear? You're taking me out for a drink with all your money?"

Geordie could tell by her slight slurring of words that she had been drinking. From *his* money, he had no doubt. And he recognised that Rosie had made a statement rather than posed a question.

"Eh," he muttered as she pushed herself off the wall, grabbed his thick hand and pulled him close.

"And of course," she murmured more loudly than she intended, "if you play your cards right, mister, and treat me *real* good, well then maybe you can not only see the goods" - she pushed his hand against her bosom, which seemed to be attempting to escape the restriction of clothing - "but get a hold of them, too."

He could smell the alcohol escaping from Rosie's mouth, but was powerless to object as she pulled him by the hand and led him through Peddie Street.

Geordie reflected how not that long ago he would have cut off his right arm to be walking down the street with this woman. But now, well now, he'd been working like a dog and risking his limbs and his life in order to get the goods for McKeany and what was he getting in return? Nothing! Nothing at all. Oh, McKeany was paying him, alright, but it was all going into the pocket of the devilish bitch who was holding his hand and leading him away like a mother pulling her wayward child out of the play area. And he, Geordie Mill, the hard man of Lochee, a gambler and a thief, could do absolutely nothing at all about it.

*

The evening itself was fine enough. The Eagle Inn was good enough, although as the evening wore on Rosie got merrier and merrier and subsequently spent more of his hard-earned shillings. By 9pm, Geordie was actually beginning to enjoy himself. A few friends turned up so he knew a card game could be organised and subsequently won. He strutted over to the two gentlemen, knowing them by face from some previous card game encounters. It didn't matter to Geordie that they were eastern European sailors - he was an open-minded gentlemen and never cared where people came from in the world, as long as he could take money from them. He held no preconceptions.

Ready for some verbal sparring, he placed his big arms around both their shoulders and said, "So, my friends. Fancy a card game in the week? The Cutty Sark is open to a deal. Unless of course, you guys are afraid?"

The larger one laughed, a deep sinister laugh that Geordie recognised as a sailor's chortle. He didn't know how or why but sailors had a set laugh. It was in their blood, perhaps to go with their gallows humour. He returned the laugh, signalling that this was time for business not bullshit. The signal was received.

"No, my friend," the sailor said to Geordie. "Me and Pad are *both* here in the week. And the Cutty Sark is right around the corner. Yes, my friend, but bring money because you will need it. Won't he, Pad?"

Geordie looked at Pad who was slightly bigger than the other sailor. He nodded his agreement. Geordie doubted whether Pad understood a word his friend had just said, but again, that was not his concern. Just then he felt warm breath on the back of his neck. It smelt of gin. Rosie was there behind him, a drink in one hand and a very sly smile on those red lips of hers. She'd broken away from the bar when Geordie was arranging his card game.

"Hi sweetie," she said. "You going to introduce me to your friends? Why…I never knew men could be so…so...big!"

As she winked towards Pad and grabbed hold of his biceps, Geordie felt anger rise up through him. He watched as Pad winked back at Rosie, his face reddening and his mouth opening to reveal just two teeth. Geordie Mill's inner beast broke through the depths of his stomach, moved into his arms and filled his fists, which he automatically clenched, pushing his fingernails into the palm of his hands until he drew blood.

The Geordie of yesteryear wouldn't have given Pad - this dumb fucking foreign sailor - a chance to show his two teeth ever again. He would have barrelled into him with balled fists and shown him that no one but *no one* messes with anything that belongs to him.

At that moment, though, Geordie Mill suddenly remembered what work he had on for tomorrow. As his blood continued to boil and his face continued to redden, he considered his long journey ahead. He'd arranged a rendezvous with his old pal, Thomas Hodge, which he hoped would lead to a hefty payment from Paul McKeany.

The partnership was working, of that there was no doubt, and Geordie simply wasn't prepared to blow it over a fucking dumb, gummy-mouthed sailor. He exhaled deeply through his nostrils and grabbed Rosie by the arm.

"Come on," he snapped, "we're out of here."

As he dragged her swiftly towards the door, her drink wobbling around in her hand, she dug her heels in and asked, "What's the problem, my dear?"

Geordie could see the two men still standing there. They were probably laughing their fucking heads off at the poor fucker whose bitch seemed to be controlling him like a fucking puppet.

He gritted his teeth, his face wrinkling like a dog's, before looking her in the eyes and saying, "You ken fine what's wrong. What's fucking wrong with you? Flirting. I'm your man, Rosie. Me...Geordie fucking Mill!"

Rosie stared back at Geordie's menacing, cold eyes and shook his hand off her arm. She once again smiled and finished her drink. Geordie felt the beast arise again.

"Well, Geordie fucking Mill," Rosie said, her voice quiet and calm. "You are taking me to the theatre next week. One of these

Shakespeare plays I've heard so much about. Because you ken what, Geordie? That new lot who call themselves the police are sniffing around for the murderer of that Mulgrew lad. There's even a reward for it. A handsome reward, Geordie. But you ken what? Why get the egg when you can get the hen!"

Geordie had no idea what the fuck she meant, but he didn't like the sound of it all the same.

"Anyway," Rosie continued nonchalantly. "Let's go home. I've had enough *fun* for one night." And with that Geordie followed her out of the Eagle Inn and towards a carriage to take them through the dirty streets of Dundee.

The evening did not get any better, which Geordie thought at the time was quite impossible. Two hours later he lay on his bed with the snoring and very rigid Rosie Trayling beside him. He wondered if his wandering hands would have any more luck this time in capturing those massive tits of hers.

They didn't.

*

The bad weather and the rickety old carriage were doing nothing for Geordie's mood, but at least the driver was a quiet type and the other passenger was an old man who could barely breathe never mind carry on a conversation. That suited Geordie just fine. If the old fella died right there and then he would simply declare he was the man's nephew and look after his body. That would save him a fucking journey and a half. It was going to be a long old ride south to Doune, but at least by the end of the week he'd be home safe and sound again. He would probably stay out there longer if he could. Give himself a rest from that crazy, demanding whore for a while, but he had to get the goods to McKeany as a matter of urgency. Business would wait for no man, unfortunately. *Anyways*, Geordie mused as the carriage rattled along, *it would be good to see his old pal Thomas Hodge again.* A little birdy had told him that Hodgey had changed his name to Thomas Stevenson. About five years ago, the men had met in the shipyards and immediately bonded. They'd shared strong booze, cheap woman and good quality tobacco together for two or three weeks, causing destruction and mischief wherever they went.

Oh, the joys of being young, Geordie reflected as the passenger next to him continued to wheeze. He remembered how Hodge had left almost as suddenly as he had arrived, and promptly had two or three burley gentlemen from the West Coast enquiring after him. Geordie assumed they weren't planning to wish him a happy birthday.

Over the past few years, Geordie had bumped into Hodgey twice, but he always seemed distracted, always a little on edge. He'd had no contact with him at all for a year then out of the blue he'd received word from one of their mutual friends that he was in Doune and living the life of a hermit, albeit with substantial savings. He was also residing next to a very peaceful burial ground called Old Kilmadock. Geordie took the information with a pinch of salt. However, the news of his old friend's location didn't sit idle in his head for long. It was time to take action. Shitting on your own doorstep was all good and well but once in a while you simply had to shit on someone else's. It was time to pay his old pal Hodge a visit.

*

After exiting the carriage, Geordie walked two miles along the north bank of the River Teith from Doune and then made his way across a large field, not feeling altogether comfortable with the sheep and dumb cows, which eyed him suspiciously.

The journey had taken him two days altogether. His passenger had not died and they had stopped off in Dunblane for an overnight stay under the trees. He was glad to be welcomed at his journey's end by his old friend Hodge, who was currently referring to himself as both Chug and Thomas Stevenson. Neither of them enquired what each other were currently up to in life, but as Geordie had brought with him a small change of clothes, some bread and a man-sized, empty black container, Geordie reckoned Hodge would reach his own conclusions. Hodge had put on weight and his beard gave Geordie the impression he wanted no one to recognise him, not even his own mother. They went back to the small barn that Chug had made home and drank some local beer that he had 'been given'. They smoked cheap snuff which he had 'won' and talked of their time on the docks and their month-long stay in Edinburgh, where they'd lodged in Tanner's Close with a loud girl named Helen McDougal and her boyfriend, William Hare.

Chug's old barn was comfortable enough and furnished with straw beds and a three-legged, wooden table propped up against the wall. Geordie also noticed a selection of tools against the far wall: spades, shovels and a menacing-looking steel bar. A collection of large, canvas bags were piled up next to an upturned wheelbarrow.

The two old friends continued to chatter like old fishwives down the pier, reminiscing about the good times they'd shared. Geordie's plan was to head to Buchany first thing in the morning, do the work and get back to the barn with the goodies. Then tomorrow he'd say his goodbyes and head home.

Simple!

Only the following day, as he reached the Old Kilmadock burial ground at St Aedh's Church, he realised he had left his box at Chug's barn. And he simply didn't have time to walk the two miles back there to fetch it.

Fuck.

He shouldn't have had so much bloody snuff last night *or* that cheap scotch in unlabelled bottles, which Hodge had mysteriously got a hold of. Damn it to damnation, there was nothing he could do about it now. Things were about to get a hell of a lot more difficult.

Geordie's breath clung to the air as he walked through the old burial ground. He realised he hadn't seen a soul for the past hour. This was the definition of the middle of nowhere. His informants were correct; this place was a free market. If only he hadn't left his fucking box at Hodge's barn he could have made this journey worth his while. Without the box he could only carry one body. Now he would have to dump his stash at the barn and take a return trip on the morrow.

Damn, damn, *damn*.

Stealing one more glance around the ground, Geordie Mill went into the old church, picked up the spade that was leaning against the back wall and headed back into the cemetery, keeping his eyes peeled for the youngest resident.

An hour and a half passed as slowly as any 90 minutes had ever gone by in Geordie Mill's life. His back ached and every time the spade scraped against a stone, a searing pain shot through his left shoulder. But as the moon once again exposed itself from the thick clouds above, Geordie hit the coffin lid and managed to prise it open. A little sweat rolled down his forehead and along his nose before dropping on the remains of an Elizabeth Duke, who had been loved and cherished by her mother, father and little brother. The body had been dressed in an ill-fitting frock and its skin was beginning to decompose. The hair, possibly once red or ginger, was now brittle white and covered most of the face, reaching down to skeletal shoulders.

The gravestone told Geordie the girl was 16 when she passed, although face-to-face with her broken body, to Geordie she could have been any age from 12 to 40.

Now it was time for the bit of hard labour he'd been dreading.

He had thrown the spade up, so it lay on the mound of earth he'd just dug up, and he leant over, grabbing the girl's dress from the side of each bosom and pulling her upwards. She resembled a disregarded rag doll sitting upwards, waiting for a little girl to come and play with her. The weight, Geordie realised, was no problem in death.

Maybe Greg could do with a slight case of death and shed some of that blubber of his, Geordie thought, attempting to lighten his mood as the now familiar stench of death entered his nostrils. Every time gas escaped from a body, it both surprised and revolted him. This time was no exception. Once the bubbly hot fart from the deceased girl was over with, Geordie stood up precariously and pulled the dead girl into a standing position. He managed to place her over his shoulder and lay her on the ground next to the spade. Puffing and panting, with sweat flowing from every pore, Geordie cursed the damn watchmen of Dundee for being extra vigilant. He'd heard it was because they were under intense pressure from the Police Force. In fact, he'd heard a rumour that these Charlies were now actually included in the force's numbers. *Damn it, they have made my life difficult,* he thought as he pushed the coffin door shut and began the slightly easier job of kicking the mound of earth back over the empty box. As he spread it flat with the sole of his boot, Geordie placed the spade back against the wall of the church and returned to the skeletal figure of Elizabeth Duke. He looked away from the headstone, which was now effectively telling a lie, and prepared to carry the goods back to the barn.

With the uneven weight of the corpse over his shoulder, Geordie stumbled every minute or two, but nevertheless continued at a steady pace over the field. He felt sick, though. He could smell rotten flesh as the corpse's buttocks occasionally rubbed against his right ear. He could feel its long hair striking his cold, sticky back. Vomit had risen in his mouth and now slid back down his throat as he trudged the two miles towards Hodge's barn. He couldn't believe he had left the fucking carrying case behind. He thought about charging McKeany extra for this one. God he was due a favour. His mind went to Rosie. Not so long ago he'd imagined her naked body locked around his. Now he wished the half-decayed corpse he was now lugging through the fields of Stirling belonged to that evil, conniving whore of a bitch. The thought made the stench and weight of it that little bit easier to handle.

A mile into his walk, just as the clouds began piling up overhead and he felt the first drops of rain strike his face, he spotted the figures of two people walking towards him. *Shit.* He looked to his left, then to his right and then to his left again, but there was nowhere to hide. There were no bushes, trees or hedgerows. Just *space*.

"Shit, shit, *shit*," Geordie said between gritted teeth. The body was hanging from his sore shoulder like an unbalanced sack. Sweat dripped quicker from his brow as he continued to stare hopelessly at the couple walking slowly towards him, blissfully unaware of the large Dundonian and the very dead young girl. Although still yards ahead, Geordie instantly felt cold. A shiver of dread surged through him as all kinds of scenarios went through his mind. The hand-in-hand couple getting a perfect description, the police rushing to the scene of the crime, finally landing an opportunity to get some much-needed results and justify the resources they'd put into finding and jailing these gravediggers. It was a win-win situation for everyone except Geordie, of course, who in two days' time could be hanging from a noose in Glasgow town centre. The last sound he'd hear would be his neck snapping and the cheering of the crowd. Rosie would no doubt be in the midst of it, Geordie's hard-earned cash squeezed in between her sweaty bosoms ready to be spent on make-up, clothes and cheap booze.

The couple were getting closer, their hands locked tightly

together. Geordie could tell from this distance they were lost in their own private world. They had their heads slightly bowed and their eyes on their feet as they kicked the damp grass below. They were gaining ground but obviously hadn't even noticed Geordie yet. He could simply drop the body and maybe pick it up in a minute or two when they were out of sight. But what if they *had* seen him? What if they stumbled across the body then saw him running in the other direction? No. There was simply only one thing to do, one course of action. *Shit, shit, shit, shit, shit.*

Geordie looked again at the pair. They were now no further than a few yards away. With a sigh he turned around and dropped young Elizabeth Duke onto her decomposing feet. As her wasted legs gave way, he hooked his arms under her armpits and pressed his hands firmly against her rotting back so he was face-to-face with her decaying corpse. He kept her in a standing position with the force of his arms and hoped desperately the couple wouldn't look at her feet, or it would appear she was levitating. Geordie may have been a good kisser, but not that good. He counted to three and prepared himself as best he could.

The couple were close now, and just about to pass Geordie and Elizabeth. It was now or never. Geordie inhaled, held his breath in his mouth and moved towards the dropped chin of Miss Duke, pushing up her face with his nose and exposing her empty eye sockets, where the smaller of God's creatures had feasted. Then he began kissing the decaying lips, sensing flecks of remaining skin fall off onto his own. He could smell the decaying flesh as it pushed up against his face and felt a slight movement in his palms where a shoulder blade clicked out of place, the skin literally falling off the bone as he continued to apply pressure. The deceased's hair lay over his shoulders as he pretended to be lost in the embrace. He could feel wisps of it move against his neck like a ghoul. Then he felt another chunk of skin, possibly an ear, fall against his face. But he continued to press his closed lips against this lifeless corpse, his eyes tight shut.

Damn it, were there still maggots in her face? Was a body this decayed going to be useable at all? And why the fuck hadn't he asked that question sooner?

He felt a squirming sensation against his lips as the stench of the corpse filled his nostrils, stimulating his gagging reflex. He kept his mouth closed as it became filled with vomit, which then found an escape route through his nose. He counted to fifty, prayed the couple had walked past him and pushed the rotten face away from his own. Still holding the corpse by its loose shoulder blades, he straightened out his arms and vomited on the grass below. Some of the yellow sick fell onto his 'companion's' dangling feet. Once the final, thick dribble had escaped from his lips, he looked behind him, relieved to see that the man and woman were still holding hands, oblivious to any misdemeanour. Geordie gave himself ten seconds to control himself, took a couple of deep breaths, used his sleeve to wipe away the vomit that was hanging from his chin and lifted the raggedy remains of Elizabeth Duke back over his throbbing shoulder for the remaining walk to Hodge's barn.

*

Slumped against the cold, damp wall of the barn, sweat and grime pinning his shirt and trousers to his cold, tired body, Geordie looked over at the body of the teenager. It was a body that he had been far more intimate with than he ever would have wished to be. He would put her in his container in a minute or so, just as soon as he had got his breath back and gathered some more energy. There was no sign of Hodge and for that Geordie was quite grateful. Quite simply, he needed to rest. *This has to be easier,* he thought. *There has to be a simpler way.*

Christ, this one job had been hellish. Fuck going out tomorrow for another body, container or no container. Maybe he would have to put up his price with McKeany. Or simply get rid of that fucking bitch Rosie. Yeah, the sex was good, but now he wasn't even getting *that*. Seeing that bitch's head on a platter would make his life easier all right. He knew he was capable of killing her. He was beginning to realise he was capable of just about anything. He closed his eyes and considered his options. This was impossible. Trips like this one were now inconceivable, but the damn Dundee police force was making it impossible to get his bodies in his home city. If it were true they had the fucking Charlies on their payroll things would be far too dangerous in the local cemeteries. *Damn it.* Damn it to hell.

As he begun to fall into unconsciousness, Geordie's brain began to tick over. His body was tired but his mind was still active. The idea came to him just as sleep got its hold. As soon as he got back to Dundee he would give Jamie and Greg a new job. A job that even those fucking morons couldn't mess up. It was a job that included a warm pub, a few pints of beer, a loose tongue and plenty of listening ears.

As Geordie Mill finally nodded off, a shadow of a smile formed on his muddy, bloodied face.

CHAPTER XII

THE JOB SEEMED easy enough to James Jeffery for once, but with Geordie Mill at the helm you never really knew where you would end up. In shit usually. Damn that fat idiot Donald McGregor for letting him get involved with such a cad. But much to his surprise, there had been no mention of the Mulgrew boy and the world seemed to have forgotten about it. For that, at least, Mill had been correct. And compared to all the effort involved in pushing wheelbarrows containing corpses, fresh and not-so-fresh, back and forth, this job did indeed *appear* to be one of the simpler ones. The Cutty Sark was busy tonight and despite it being a Friday, the atmosphere was tense. Success and money came with its own problems and this was felt keenly in the dockside bar. Jamie could already hear mumblings about the useless police force being fit for nothing, the gangs of kids who were working the dockyards, the cesspits of waste that were invading the streets, the stench of boiling whale blubber, the cramped conditions, the unemployment, the burglaries, the rapes and the body snatching. Sleep had not taken Jamie in its embrace since that fateful night in Jessman's Court. He glanced around at the tavern's punters and could smell a mixture of hops, sweat and tobacco. The place seemed anxious, on edge somehow. Indeed, Mill had picked his time and place well. He might have been a dangerous, violent man but as Jamie looked around at the drinkers who were all angry with the world, he had to concede that he knew what he was doing.

Whilst Jamie stood uncomfortably near a mean-looking gaggle of dockworkers while awaiting Greg, he shuffled from foot to foot in nervous anticipation. Geordie had bought him a drink last night, a miracle in itself, and told him what to do. A little money had passed between them and then Geordie was gone. For that Jamie was pleased. He looked *fucking* awful and had smelt even worse. He didn't ask. He wasn't a *complete* idiot.

Greg walked towards Jamie, squeezing through the crowds with difficulty, two tankards of ale in his bulky hands.

He passed Greg his drink and the pair got to work.

"Bloody hell, Greg," said Jamie a little louder than usual. "I can't fucking believe what I saw when I walked past the Logie Cemetery, you ken, the one on the Lochee Road."

"Aye."

"And you know the two watchmen they have on duty?"

Greg nodded with large, exaggerated movements.

Christ, thought Jamie. *These Shakespeare actors must be quaking in their fucking boots.*

Acting certainly wasn't in Donald McGregor's blood. But he kept his opinion to himself as they continued with their plan.

"Well, I walked past, not ten minutes ago, and they were *fast asleep!*"

"FAST ASLEEP! No way!"

"Aye, fast asleep."

"I can't fucking believe that the watchmen at the LOGIE cemetery were FAST ASLEEP! What if...God forbid, something should happen..."

"I ken, Greg. It's disgusting. They're fast asleep I'm telling you. FAST ASLEEP!"

Greg and Jamie then scuttled to another part of the Cutty Sark and found a place to stand next to a table where five card players were seated with a Welsh prostitute they knew as Gobbler. Greg assumed the card players worked in one of the mills further uptown. It was another good spot.

"Bloody hell, Greg," said Jamie as loudly as before. "I can't fucking believe what I saw when I walked past the Logie Cemetery, you ken, the one on the Lochee Road."

"Aye."

"And you know the two watchmen they have on duty? Well, I walked past, not ten minutes ago, and they were *fast asleep!*"

"FAST ASLEEP! No way!"

"Aye, fast asleep!"

"I can't fucking believe that the watchmen at the LOGIE Cemetery were FAST ASLEEP! What if…God forbid, something should happen…"

"I ken, Greg. It's disgusting. They're fast asleep I'm telling you. FAST ASLEEP!"

They shook their heads at the thought of such atrocity and then walked through the bustling tavern to find another location.

And so on.

And so on.

As their second lap was taking place, Jamie and Greg witnessed first-hand how gossip was repeated, altered, manipulated and used as a tool for people's anger and frustration. Jamie wasn't quite sure what Mill was up to at first, but now he'd overheard the conversations, felt the anger generated and witnessed the ill feeling around him building, he'd got an inkling of what it was that devious bastard had devised. More people would get hurt, that was for sure. He waited for Greg to come back from his piss and took a deep breath. What the fuck did he expect from Geordie Mill anyway?

As the pair finished off their last paid-for drinks, all sorts of snippets were reaching their ears from around them.

"Do you ken there were two gravediggers getting to work on a grave while two Charlies slept next to them?"

"Did you hear that two fucking Charlies drank themselves to oblivion while fucking gravediggers dug up the body of a wee bairn right *next* tae them?"

"I heard that the gravediggers are *actually* buying the Charlies the booze. And the Charlies are accepting it!"

"And snuff."

"Aye, and snuff."

"Whores?"

"*Whores*?"

"Aye, probably whores too!"

"Let's get doon to the Logie Cemetery, sort oot these lazy, drunken Charlies!"

"Aye, let's go."

"Aye."

Jamie and Greg watched as at least 15 angry men walked out of the Sark, headed for Logie Cemetery, where they intended to wake up the drunk, sleeping, double-crossing criminal Charlies who were now probably standing on guard, bright-eyed, bushytailed and doing a fine job of defending the deceased. Jamie hoped they could run fast and felt a pang of guilt. Of course, it was going to end in bloodshed. This *was* the brainchild of Geordie bloody Mill after all. With an emotion that Jamie couldn't quite put his finger on - possibly guilt, possibly remorse, possibly regret - he decided he better get over to the cemetery to see what was happening first-hand. Anyway, he was sure Geordie would want to know the result of his deviousness.

*

A crowd of 20 or so had already formed at the entrance of the cemetery when Jamie arrived there with Greg. Through the darkness, Jamie could see the two watchmen holding their lanterns aloft and alighting their faces so they were in full view of the mob.

"Do your job and stop sleeping!" Jamie heard one of the angry men shout.

"What?" the Charlie replied. "Who says we're sleeping? We've never slept on the job!"

"Liar," shouted someone else.

Guilt began to eat away at Jamie's conscience.

"I am not!" shouted the defiant Charlie over the cemetery walls.

"Prove it!" said another voice.

"How?"

Jamie could see a look of anger, confusion and pride on the poor Charlie's face. He was obviously wondering what the fuck was happening.

"I dinna ken. How aboot you shout out the minutes. Then we'll ken if you're sleeping or no."

The suggestion was followed by a mumble of approval by all. Well, everyone except the two watchmen. In fact, they looked like they had just eaten a fishing hook.

"You what?" shouted the other Charlie. And then, before the mob could answer, he added a defiant, "Fuck off!"

It was not the wisest of retorts. One of the mob split from the crowd and headed for the cemetery. Jamie recognised him as one of the shipyard workers from the Cutty Sark. He watched as if the scene was taking place in front of him in slow motion. The shipyard worker snatched the watchmen's lantern from his hand and slammed it on the ground below. The sound echoed through the cemetery and the mob fell momentarily silent as the action unfolded. As quick as a flash, the watchman tensed his fist and punched the dockworker square in the face.

Watching him fall to the ground with a thud stirred the rest of the crowd into action. They shouted, screamed and ran for the cemetery. It was twenty versus two. As any gambler would conclude, the odds were not in the Charlies' favour. They never stood a chance…

CHAPTER XIII

As McKeany looked up and glanced out towards the packed room in front of him, he knew his moment had finally arrived. Over a hundred young faces sat in the lecture hall, most of them awaiting their first anatomy lesson. They had just taken a mighty step closer to achieving their dream. A job as a surgeon was well paid and well respected and would provide them with the opportunity to take all that was needed from life. And they were about watch Dr McKeany's dissection, listen to his understanding of the human body and spread the word that the best anatomist in Britain was right here in the industrial hub of Dundee.

McKeany was waiting for his assistant, Jacob, one of his ex students, to bring in the fresh, young body. He knew that Edinburgh and London were struggling. In both these big cities, *The Medical Times* reported that the resurrection men were demanding 'finishing money'. This meant that if they were unfortunate enough to get a term of imprisonment, the teacher hiring them had to agree to partly keep the man's wife and family fed whilst he was behind bars. McKeany had also heard rumours that in Edinburgh, resurrectionists maintained their monopoly by calling the police if one of their clients chose someone else to fetch their 'goods'. With Geordie Mill on his side, McKeany felt like he had landed squarely on his feet. He did his job *well*. Yes, maybe he was a little rough round the edges, but McKeany already had nine fresh bodies in his outhouse and another currently scrubbed up and under a white cloth ready to be wheeled in for dissection. McKeany reckoned his future had only just begun.

With a detectable sense of theatre, Jacob handed his tools to McKeany as the doctor lectured about the organ system, showing his startled audience the lungs, heart, kidneys and stomach. The young students oohed and aahed as McKeany held the heart in his hands and described how each and every organ was connected to each other, just like God's will was connected to all of us.

After 40 minutes, the students were on their feet applauding. McKeany could see Dr Macraig-Robinson at the back of the auditorium nodding his approval. As Jacob wheeled out the remains of the carcass, McKeany had his first taste of success. As he took a bow he was sure it would not be his last. The audience responded in kind.

*

In McKeany's opinion, the second autopsy was even better than the first and now his third one of the week had just finished to another standing ovation. He walked out of the school to be greeted by a gaggle of students, some members of the press, a tall, lanky man from *The Medical Times* and a number of young, pretty ladies. Whilst their admiration of the sciences was questionable, their adoration of tomorrow's celebrity was clear. As McKeany hustled his way through the crowd to his carriage, he spotted Dr Fairborough talking to Dr Macraig-Robinson. Who would have known they were friends? Fairborough was standing tall and looking very proud next to the older man. Meanwhile, questions were being fired at him thick and fast.

"Doctor McKeany, when's your next lecture?"

"Doctor McKeany, how are the lungs and heart connected – through blood or through the soul?"

"Doctor McKeany, will you still practice in Dundee when you are bigger than Doctor Robert Knox? Why don't you join the Institute? Will the autopsies be thrice a week all term?"

As he attempted to answer each question and reached out to shake the hands being offered to him, McKeany noticed his father-in-law slicing through the crowd like a sharp cutting wire. His intimidating figure was making light work of the masses.

"Ah, Paul," he said, "Dear son, Dr Macraig-Robinson here was just saying what an *outstanding* talent you are. Well, it's no surprise to me, of course. I always knew that. But come, would you like to go for a quick drink with your father-in-law? I know dear Charlotte will be dying to have you home but I'm sure she won't mind."

"Eh…" McKeany stuttered, "okay".

"Good," Doctor Fairborough replied. "Let's go back to my house. Mrs Fairborough will be *so* glad to see you. It's been way too long."

And with that he gently led his son-in-law into the carriage and away from the adoring crowd.

"Don't worry, son. They'll still be there next week," Dr Fairborough said as they departed. "You're a celebrity now."

Paul McKeany beamed as the horse and cart trotted towards the large houses of West Ferry.

CHAPTER XIV

GEORDIE PLACED HIS newspaper down on the table and wondered why all the people in the world were so bloody stupid. If the world were full of Mills it would be superior, strong, neat and in full working order. Nothing would break, nothing would malfunction, nothing would die. Things would run as smooth as clockwork. The truth of the matter, however, was that there were idiots all around him and these idiots could well put him under pressure, *despite* all the hard graft he'd been putting into his new career. The newspaper article he'd just read explained the arrest of a Bishop and May in Edinburgh, and their subsequent death sentence. The men had travelled down to London and attempted to sell a body to Guy's Hospital for 12 guineas, but they had been refused. They then offered it to a Mr Grainger at his Anatomical Theatre, but they were turned down once more. Finally, they attempted to flog it to King's College, where the porter was suspicious and alerted the authorities. It was found to be the body of an Italian boy named Carlo Ferrari. He'd made his living from entertaining street crowds with his white mice collection. The boy's teeth had been extracted and previously sold to Mr Cameron, a dentist. The jury found all three men guilty of murder. It was dolts like these that made Geordie Mill's life that bit harder. He was thankful that unlike Bishop and May, he was cleverer than the average gravedigger, burker, murderer and jury. It took brains *and* stealth to make it in this business and that was exactly why he, Geordie Mill, was finally experiencing success in his life.

The riot at the Logie Cemetery had gone exactly to plan. Between them, the two watchmen had sustained a broken leg, a broken wrist, a broken nose each and a number of tooth losses.

You have to break a few eggs to make an omelette, Geordie thought smugly.

The system was crumbling. The people didn't trust the Charlies and the Charlies didn't trust the people. The Police Force was being repositioned to watch out for both over-zealous Charlies and het-up crowds hanging around the cemeteries. This gave Geordie a little breathing space to collect and deliver a few more bodies to McKeany, who, in his defence, was paying him sweetly and punctually. When the bodies were delivered to his outhouse there was always a small envelope waiting in the right hand corner containing Mill's payment. No name, no note, just money. Nothing more, nothing less. Mill was also thankful that McKeany had an ounce of intelligence, too. It was indeed a partnership made in heaven.

Geordie began readying himself for his evening's work. Rosie had been unusually quiet for the last few days and rumour had it she had a terrible cough and was laid up in bed. Geordie wished for a slow recovery. It would at least give him the opportunity to work tonight in peace and quiet, and maybe spend his profit before her beady fucking eyes saw it and drank it all away.

He tied the laces of his boots up tight, pulled on his torn gloves, put on his jacket and set out from his lodgings to walk the streets of Dundee. He looked like a man with a mission and he knew exactly where he was heading. He had been checking her out for the last three evenings.

*

Geordie grinned like a shark when he saw her. She'd turned up, regular as clockwork, at her usual spot on the filth and urine-riddled cobbled streets. Geordie noted her eyes darting furiously left to right, right to left in ready anticipation of the taverns closing and business picking up. As Geordie walked towards her, he couldn't help thinking about Rosie. He wondered why the fuck he just didn't do to her what he was about to do to this whore, who named herself Petal. Unless her mother and father saw flowers as wilted, saggy, desperate, rancid, stinking and defeated creatures, Geordie assumed the name was a made up one. No doubt she was attempting to sound different, exotic even. To Geordie it simply sounded cheap and desperate. He walked up to Petal, collar tight against his thick neck, hands tight in his pockets and produced his best smile.

"Hello, Petal, darling."

"Oh, hi, Geordie. You looking for Rosie?"

"She's ill, I heard," Geordie replied. He realised he was shaking a little. Was it nerves, anticipation, excitement? He couldn't put his finger on what it was, but he still couldn't stop grinning. Maybe it was a smile of pride at the absolute foolproof idea he'd constructed.

"Yeah," Petal said, her lips as bright as blood.

Geordie noted she had stuffed her top with material to hide her malnutrition. "She's in a bad way, Geordie. She's staying at Sallie's up Peddie Street. You should really pay her a visit, you know."

Geordie shrugged, yet tried to appear caring. "Yeah I ken. I will do."

Geordie attempted his sad puppy-eyed look. He was beginning to wonder if this acting malarkey paid well. If so he could go on to be the richest man this side of town.

"Aye," Petal answered. Geordie noted a slight twinkle in her dull brown eyes.

"And y'ken well, let's say, I've came in tae a bit of money."

The twinkle appeared a little brighter. Petal leaned forward a little. He noticed a blue vein on her neck, which looked as if it was attempting to escape through her pale skin, which itself was attempting to escape the puddle of make-up that had been caked on top of it.

"Aye."

"Well," Geordie said, mastering his timid look. "The thing is, you see – well, I have money in ma pocket and well, I haven't had it in a couple of weeks and y'ken, a man has…has…"

"Needs?"

"Aye, needs," Geordie replied. As his face twitched he tried to hide his smile with his hand and look coy. The fish had been hooked.

"Well, Geordie," Petal said, squeezing her bosoms together and desperately trying to push them up. "I'm a friend of Rosie y'ken and it doesn't sit right with me, but for a friend I suppose."

With that, Petal moved her hand towards Geordie's belt and pulled him towards her.

Geordie wilfully kept his hands in his pockets and attempted to fake a sexually excited smile. He hoped it didn't show as a grimace. Christ, as long as they paid well he *must* be in one of these bloody theatre plays.

"Not here, Petal. I mean, I wouldn't…*we* wouldn't want Rosie finding out, right?"

"Eh…right," Petal agreed, removing her talon-like hands, "you got somewhere in mind?"

"Oh yeah," said Geordie smiling. There was no faking this one - it was a 100 per cent genuine.

The fish had not only been hooked, it was about to be boned, skinned, boiled and sold.

*

Geordie glanced behind him one last time, just to make certain that no unwanted eyes had followed him here. Then he led Petal into the back alley leading to Paul McKeany's outhouse. He took out the key from his trouser pocket and clicked it into the padlock, unlocking it with one swift movement. The door clicked open and Mill gently led Petal inside the wooden shed.

"Oh my god, it stinks in here," she said and then gave Geordie a sneaky smile. "What *is* this place?"

Geordie squinted through the fading light, adjusting his eyes to the dark. A lantern was illuminating the street outside and although it was enough to highlight the shapes in the room, it wasn't enough to light up its finer details.

Geordie didn't particularly want to light the lantern hanging from the ceiling, but a part of him felt the need to witness Petal's final minutes in this world. For one reason or another, it was imperative for her to know that Geordie Mill was not just your typical man but as smart and as cunning as the Devil himself. He thought of Petal laughing with Rosie as the latter told her how he wasn't a real man like that pock-marked Polish sailor she used to fuck. Or maybe she'd informed Petal of her plans to blackmail him and spend all of his money.

No, he had to see this. And anyway, if McKeany's wife saw the light on he was sure she wouldn't bat an eye. He recalled the doctor telling him that she didn't give a shit about his business. All she cared about was *his* money and *her* friends. He remembered thinking that it didn't matter what side of the fence you were on, women were still fucking women. Whores, the whole fucking stinking lot of them. Just some had more camouflage than others.

"Just my *secret little place*," Geordie replied as he struck a match and lit the lantern. Petal removed her hands from her face, her long, crooked fingers reaching for Geordie's trousers.

"Oh well, each to their own, eh?" she said as she grasped hold of his belt. "So, how do you like it?"

Geordie swiped away Petal's hands and looked her in the eyes. "So, what's Rosie been saying?"

Petal looked up at Geordie and wiped away some stray red hairs from her thin face. "Rosie? Why are you talking about Rosie?"

She paused then made for his belt again. She quite obviously wanted to get this job done and dusted. In and out, so to speak.

Geordie pushed away her hands again, more forcibly this time. Petal took a step back, falling over a pile of old cloth. As her hands broke her fall, she felt a soft substance beneath her palms. A squelching sound could be heard as she applied more pressure to it, desperately seeking leverage to get back on her feet. The smell was now overpowering.

"What, what *is* this place?" she asked as a naked arm protruded from below the cloth and swung down. Geordie couldn't afford for her to scream. He picked her up by her hair and looked into her defeated, bloodshot brown eyes one final time before grabbing her head and twisting her neck until a snapping sound filled the outhouse. Then he let her fall onto the three dead bodies that Mckeany had yet to have delivered to his school.

Reaching up, he grabbed a large roll of cloth from the shelf and threw it over her. Then he leant over to the far side of the outhouse and picked up the plain envelope containing his payment. Good old reliable McKeany.

"Not even a barrow needed," he said to himself, remembering the mess Bishop and May had gotten into in Edinburgh. "That's how you do it, boys," he added, as he put out the light with his finger and his thumb.

Exiting the outhouse, he locked it behind him and walked down the street towards his lodgings. *Sometimes*, he thought to himself, *life is just a little too easy.*

He found himself whistling an old sea shanty as he patted the payment in his jacket pocket. This one was going to be spent by him, and *him* alone.

*

This time, Paul McKeany didn't notice the light glowing from inside his outhouse. On the last three occasions Geordie had delivered the goods, he'd stood at the side of the window out of view and watched as the large man wheeled what looked like a sack of potatoes into the outhouse before walking out with an empty wheelbarrow.

At first, McKeany did this because of his innate distrust of the aggressive and large commoner. He had never mixed with his type before. Yes, he was aware of how the other half lived, but studious intellects like himself didn't usually have cause to come into contact with the burley rough men who gambled, fought and drank. It was just the way the world worked. Just lately, McKeany had been keeping watch out of sheer curiosity. He also knew that when a delivery was made it was easier to arrange the pick up as soon as possible, before the stench got too much and suspicion was raised. His curiosity also had another function. Standing at the window helped block Charlotte's view, just in case she looked out and saw their outhouse inhabited. However, McKeany knew he was just being over cautious. In fact, he wondered if Charlotte even knew the outside shed belonged to them. And even if she did, quite frankly, did she give a shit? McKeany knew the answer to that one too. As the outhouse didn't involve jewelley, make-up or gossip, it was a firm no.

However, McKeany wasn't at the window for an entirely new reason. After arriving home from his father-in-law's house and spending an hour or so being lavished with praise, Mr Fairborough kept him company on the carriage ride home and stopped off for a dram of whisky so he could vocalise that same praise to his daughter. He continually recounted just how the crowd had idolised her husband, how he was the talk of the town and how skilled he was in anatomy.

"I knew your husband was talented, Charlotte, but just *how* talented, well I never. What a mind and how knowledgeable he is!"

"Oh, I know, father," Charlotte had replied. McKeany listened out for the sarcastic notes but didn't detect any. "He is *so* intelligent. I *always* tell my friends that."

Paul McKeany gleamed with pride. Dr Fairborough beamed with pride. And Charlotte McKeany beamed with pride at the thought of her celebrity husband. And after Dr Fairborough departed, Charlotte looked at her husband in a way McKeany had never witnessed before. Was she ill? Her eyes widened and she leant over to kiss his nose, before very slowly and very delicately lowering her lips to his.

Although very used to it, McKeany didn't particularly want to risk another rejection, but he took the gamble and grabbed hold of Charlotte's hand. This time her fingers entwined with his and she led him to the master bedroom.

And that was why McKeany missed seeing the man and woman entering his outhouse and a lone man exiting it a few minutes later. Because, for the first time in his life, McKeany was, as the commoners put it, balls deep inside his wife.

God, Paul McKeany loved this high life. Life was sweet and by jove he was enjoying every single minute of it. After possibly the best four minutes of his entire life, he collapsed onto his back, with Charlotte lying peacefully on his chest. He could feel goosebumps prickle as the sweat from his recent exertion evaporated over his naked body. As sleep took its comforting, post-coital hold, Paul McKeany relaxed like an innocent infant in his mother's arms.

CHAPTER XV

JOHN WILSON FELT content in the knowledge that God would be very proud of his right-hand man. He sipped his tea slowly, savouring the sweet brew. His chair sat in a corner of his sparse new lodgings, which were situated in a busy part of the town. Yes, of course there was a part of him that wished he was in the quieter part of Dundee, the more civilised section, maybe Broughty or the West End, but his maker had put him here in this shitehole for a reason. He knew he should be proud of being the one chosen to bring justice to this squalid neighbourhood next to Coutties Wynd. Outside his window, the noise of carts travelling across granite cobbles and the clatter of machinery from the neighbouring factories did little to hide the calls of starving children, beggars and drunks. He inhaled deeply, took another sip of his tea and reflected on yesterday's work.

The Polish dockworker was easy. The large man readily accepted the tobacco from the generous local. Wilson wondered if he managed to get back to his lodgings in time for the drug to take effect. Scratching out your own eyes and attempting to itch your throat until it snapped must be uncomfortable, especially if you hadn't reached the comfort of your own bed.

Well, serves the foreigners right for coming over here and polluting this land, John decided.

However, it was the woman who had caused him most concern. He knew it was his own fault because he'd made a weak batch. At first he'd considered throwing the tobacco away for the rodents to consume, but then he decided to make do and make three cigarettes from it. Anyway, the ensuing death would be just as definite, maybe just a little slower. He would simply have to be a little careful who the participants were. He was not ready to risk getting caught by the shambles they were calling the Police Force.

Anyway, the prostitute was perfect. And it was worth the money for the hand job, although her hands were disgusting to the touch. Afterwards, she lit up her cigarette and walked back down towards the Overgate. At the same time, John Wilson zipped up his trousers, walked to his lodgings, scrubbed his penis with hot water until it stung and put a brew on. He wondered if the filthy bitch would suffer. He sincerely hoped she would.

*

As Paul McKeany recalled the hollers, cheers and roaring applause from a couple of hours ago, his penis became even harder. He couldn't recall it being this stiff since he was a teenager.

Charlotte was groaning with ecstasy beneath him, her pale body writhing under his sweaty one, her lips pursed and searching for a kiss, her eyelashes fluttering away as he entered her more deeply.

McKeany's eyes rolled to heaven as he was filled with pleasure.

McKeany's beautiful wife had been part of the audience tonight. She'd stood next to her father as he'd lifted out the heart, slicing it delicately and displaying clearly the separate four chambers and its door-like valves connecting the bloody segments. She was there, looking at her father's reaction as the medical students oohed and aahed at the body of a man being dissected in front of them. She watched McKeany slice up more organs and present them like trophies. She witnessed the dreamy look on the faces of the students, who all fantasised about being an intellectual powerhouse like their lecturer one day. He was pushing the boundaries of the natural sciences.

Following the lecture, once he had washed up, thanked his assistant and walked out of the main door of the theatre, Charlotte was there to witness McKeany being bombarded with questions by the students.

And now, more than an hour later, here he was in bed with his beloved. What they were doing couldn't even be described as lovemaking - they were mating like a pair of wild chimpanzees. McKeany pushed his hands flat against the mattress as Charlotte groaned in delight under him. For a second he stole a glance outside and saw the smog attempt to cover the half moon. As he reached climax, McKeany felt the day's hard work wash away from him in a sea of calm and satisfaction.

*

The dirty, damp room was going in and out of focus as Rosie wondered where her friend Petal had gone. Her back and tits felt bruised, her throat was as dry as a bone and her head felt like it was being squashed by a whaling ship. Although her eyesight had adjusted to the dark, she continually mistook the clothes hanging over her door for a man - a man who would soon take her to the other side. So this is what death felt like. The sweat from her body stank and drenched the mattress, yet she still felt as cold as ice. She wasn't sure if she had shit herself or not. Was this the plague? How on earth did she catch it? Was this God's revenge for being a whore? Her last job with the slightly older man was only last night. Or was it last week? Last month? Her fever knocked out time and entwined with her physical discomfort, leaving her feeling confused. Was this the work of Geordie Mill? The idea came and went and she desperately wished that Petal or even Geordie would walk through the door and give her the medicine she desperately craved.

Snot trailed from her nose as drool hung from her open lips. Rosie Trayling sobbed in the empty room and shivered. She now knew for certain that Death was her next punter.

*

Geordie Mill was on his second ale of the evening. The first one had barely touched the sides and James Jeffrey and Donald McGregor were feeling a tad uneasy. Geordie Mill in a bad mood may have been uncomfortable and tense, but Geordie Mill in a jovial mood was quite simply unheard of. They figured that something was most definitely wrong.

"Come on, boys," he said as the ale flowed down his large mouth. "Next one's on me."

The two men stole a glance at one another and hid behind their tankards. Was this a trick? Was Geordie planning to ply them with alcohol then smash in their skulls and dump them in that outhouse? Greg's jowls shook slightly at the thought of this and he glanced once more at Jamie.

Jamie got the message and took the lead.

"So, eh, Geordie…eh, why, why, why are you in such a good…good mood. I mean, you're usually in a good…good mood, but…"

Geordie plopped down his drink, looked straight at Jamie's lean face and laughed. Geordie baring his teeth reminded Jamie of a demented horse.

"My friends," he said, slapping both men across the back, "let's just say business is good and…"

Just then a young Irish woman slowly approached the table. She looked timid, scared even.

"Eh, Geordie Mill?" she enquired. Her Dublin accent was

very strong and she was rubbing her hands together and shuffling her feet.

"Yes, that is me," Geordie said smiling. "I recognise you, you're one of Rosie's crew, aye?"

"Yeah," she said slowly. "That's why I'm here, to tell you how sorry I am. The plague, Geordie, it took poor Rosie."

With that, the young girl ran out of the tavern in a flood of tears.

Jamie and Greg looked down at their ales, their heads bowed. Awaiting all sorts of reactions, they gave it ten or so seconds before braving a glimpse at Geordie. His eyes looked a little sad but his teeth were still displaying that dangerous, horse-like grin.

"Fuck it," he said. "She was just a whore after all. Let's get another drink." With that he stood up and walked to the bar.

But, as he reached it, he suddenly felt a surge of very strange emotions indeed. Rosie was *his*, his partner if you will, his lover, but she had chosen a dangerous path by blackmailing him. The irony was that Mother Nature had killed her and not his own large hands. He ordered his drinks and pondered how even the world was now on his side.

He was due to collect another body from the dock tomorrow. This one was a Polish migrant who didn't have any family. Maybe after that he could fit in another two quick killings. Then he could give himself a break, perhaps take a holiday to Edinburgh to catch up with a few pals.

Things, Geordie decided, had never been better.

Extract from *The Aberdeen Journal, 1825*:

The City of DUNDEE is finally competing with its rivals in the academic hubs of EDINBURGH and GLASGOW in the MEDICAL SCIENCES. Although recently appointed as

Fellow of the Royal Society of Edinburgh on a salary of nearly £100, Doctor Robert Knox is being put under pressure for his recent introduction of the theory of transcendental anatomy. The flamboyant Knox is still bringing in the crowds for his squeamish lectures and still full of wit and wonder whilst dressed in his overgown and showing off his bloody fingers, BUT reports from one of his three assistants record he is concerned about 'activities on the east coast.'

These activities in the east coast have arrived in the guise of a local teacher named PAUL MCKEANY. MCKEANY is reported to be an outstanding anatomist and teacher, less flamboyant than Knox but - as recent reports state - "far more modest with theories which every man can relate to". Medical students are simply flocking to catch one of the lectures by MCKEANY who teaches whilst the dissection is carried out in an educational manner. Naturally the comparisons between Knox and McKeany may be superficial, but the anatomists could not be more contrasting. Knox who was remembered as a bully and who won the Provost's medal in his final year at the Royal High School is indeed very different to McKeany, who is a modest man, with quiet, timid tendencies and seemed to attend school in Dundee with a studious but a very quiet nature. It also seems that McKeany's method of collecting cadavers is sound and ethical, a statement sometimes not echoed when regarding Knox's practice. As medical students flock to the east coast, some EXPERTS are talking of a medical boom in DUNDEE as well as in LONDON and EDINBURGH.

CHAPTER XVI

"**M**ADAM, MAY I have this dance?"

Charlotte McKeany blushed as she giggled and accepted her husband's hand. As he led her across the dance floor she stared into his eyes, ever aware of the eyes upon them. Some of the onlookers were proud, some were interested and some were damn right jealous of her husband's success. It had been a wonderful evening in which she had sat next to her cousin, Betsy, and eaten the finest food the Tay Hotel could offer - seafood fit for royalty and bubbles fit only for the cream of society. The other wines were also exquisite. This was *indeed* where she belonged. As they'd dined she'd answered questions on her husband's success.

"Did you *always* know he was a talented man?"

"Did you fall in love with his brains or his brawn?"

"Did you *know* that all the young women want to know where you buy your clothes from?"

"Oh yes," Charlotte replied to the first question. After all, of course she knew her husband had it in him. She had always known it was only a matter of time. And she'd been attracted to *both* his brains *and* his brawn. And people wanting to know where she shopped was just silly.

"I'm just an average woman," she said. "It is *my husband* who is the special one."

Attention was being piled on her like a thick carpet. Charlotte

McKeany was now a social butterfly and she loved *every* single minute of it.

And Paul McKeany soon realised that the more attention she attained from the masses, the more she gave back to him, which was indeed a result.

And, as he clumsily attempted to glide her around the dance floor, Charlotte reflected on how it didn't matter if he wasn't the most handsome man in the room or indeed the most graceful. It was, after all, *his* name on everyone's lips. He *was* the man of the moment and Charlotte knew it. She also knew that this made her the lady of the moment.

McKeany stole a few glances at the surrounding guests who were politicians, judges and businessman: men with wealth, prestige and *power*. He saw Charlotte steal a glance at her cousin who was sitting at one of the tables enjoying some attention. He continued to hold his wife tight as he thought about his next lecture and the ever-increasing demand for tickets to see him perform his magic. The world was indeed a good place and Dr Paul McKeany was finally reaping life's best rewards. As his father had once taught him, hard work *does* eventually pay off.

CHAPTER XVII

GEORDIE'S BACK AND neck ached but he was on a roll and, as God knew, until the dice stopped landing in your favour you should never stopped rolling the bastard. He walked the streets looking for patterns, finding people with the same routines and hunting down the empty spaces...the ones so quiet that no one would hear a thud, shout, yelp or a scream. He measured the distance between these quiet streets and McKeany's outhouse, calculating the distance, the gradient and the ease of delivery.

Over the last three weeks, Geordie Mill had worked the local area and discovered every nook and cranny and identified every slow-witted, retarded, small, old or senile potential victim. He'd read all about McKeany's success and knew all about his celebrity status and the balls and parties he and his wife had attended with other renowned guests.

McKeany and Mill hadn't met face-to-face since that evening in the safe house, and for this Mill was grateful. Things were sweet as a nut and changing the plan now would be disastrous. The outhouse, delivery and payment – in and out. *Easy*. Mill was glad of McKeany's success. It relied on Mill's and they would make each other rich. Synergy and synchronicity. One in the limelight, one out of it. Mill was more than happy with that. It was the way of the world. He didn't belong in a place of learning just as much as McKeany didn't belong in his world of fights and fucking down Horses Wynd. He continued to survey the local area, although he was pretty sure tomorrow he would deliver another specimen. It was nature in a way. After all, if you were willing to walk the *same* quiet streets at the *same* time every night then you deserved to run into a spot of bother.

*

There was no doubt Norma was a creature of habit. Every early evening she went to Morag's house for a quick natter and a game of bridge. But if Norma stayed any longer than half an hour, Morag started to get confused and a little short tempered. *Poor Morag*, thought Norma. *Five years ago she had a great mind and a sharp wit to go with it.*

The past few years had seen her lose her husband and her beautiful, 20-year-old daughter, and this had taken its toll.

On some days when Norma visited it was like talking to the Morag of old. On others she may as well have been talking to a stranger. Dear, dear Morag. Norma took comfort in the fact she could talk to Albert about Morag's progress. An accident in the dockyard had left him bedridden, but despite his own struggles he was a great listener – always had been. And although Morag wasn't fully herself today, Albert would indeed be pleased to hear how she was getting on.

When Norma left Morag's home and turned the corner, she walked right into the path of a very well-dressed gentleman. Norma promptly dropped her bag containing the nice loaf of bread she'd bought to share with Albert later. The man dropped a little sachet of tobacco. Once apologies were exchanged and everything had been picked up, Norma and the gentleman, a well-educated man called John, chatted for four or five minutes. Norma told him about her poorly husband and Mr Wilson listened with a sympathetic look on his face. As they departed company, the kind stranger presented Norma with the small pouch of tobacco he had dropped to give to her bed-ridden spouse. Norma smiled, said her thanks and walked towards home. She relished the thought of her husband enjoying the treat of some good tobacco and a nice slice of toasted bread. The kindness of strangers lifted her spirits as she clutched the unexpected gift in her hand.

*

Forty-eight hours after Geordie had last scouted for connections, he found himself leaning against the same lamppost in the same quiet street in the same quiet part of town. He was acclimatising to the stench of whale blubber, which was particularly strong in the air tonight.

Right on time there she was again. The elderly woman was shuffling home, this time with her hand clasped around something. Geordie noticed the smile on her face. It made him happier to think she had experienced joy on her final day in this world.

He looked around again, checking and double-checking that the street remained as quiet as it had been. It should be, he'd observed it enough bloody times over the past weeks. He then checked that his wheelbarrow was where it should be, against the wall with two grey blankets large enough for a body. Perfect.

He boldly pushed himself away from the wall he was leaning against and walked confidently in the same direction as the smiling old lady who'd shuffled past him not 30 seconds earlier. *It was a quick, slick move, a move,* Geordie mused, *that a man half his age and size would have been proud of.*

As he stepped in behind her, the woman realised there was a large shadow behind her, but before she could turn around, Geordie's large hand extended out and folded around her thin, skeletal neck. He applied some pressure before twisting it until it snapped. At this point, Geordie noticed that the thing she was carrying was a little pouch of snuff. He was delighted by the added bonus of a good smoke. After all, this killing was hard work.

He dropped the body onto the ground. As Norma fell, her slack fingers dropped the pouch and her lifeless leg swung around and kicked it down the cobbled, wet road.

Damn it, thought Geordie as he raced to recover the waiting wheelbarrow. This was the most stressful part, the unattended body risk. He quickly collected it and shoved Norma in head and shoulders first, folding her legs at the knees in order to fit in her whole body. Then he covered her with the blankets and looked around for the pouch of tobacco. It was nowhere to be seen.

"Can't a man get *some* luck in this town?" he quietly asked the deceased Norma.

Feeling slightly dejected, he straightened the blankets and pushed the barrow towards the home of Dundee's new celebrity doctor.

*

Back at the outhouse, Geordie tipped the old woman onto another body.

Body? Surely there must be more than one left? Geordie thought.

He wiped the sweat from his brow, ensured the body was completely covered and looked for the unmarked envelope with his payment inside. As always, McKeany hadn't let him down. Just as he was about to place the envelope safely in his inside pocket, he noticed a small note written on it. It simply said:

G. Bo Lo

G. Bo Lo? Geordie thought as he locked up the outhouse and placed the wheelbarrow back where it belonged.

G.Bo.Lo? Geordie Bo low down, Geordie bo load? Geordie, bo…body..bodies lo…low – That's it. Geordie bodies low! There was only one after all, and Geordie knew how successful McKeany's lectures had been. He had been reading the newspaper after all – mainly because he was curious about how the hunt for the Mulgrew boy's killer was going and wanted to check up on the developments (or not) of the new Dundee Police Force. Fucking donkeys, the lot of them. Even the press agreed. He sneaked a glance up at the house but noticed it was dark. All the lights were off. Either the inhabitants had gone to bed early or they were out somewhere celebrating their new success.

Geordie wondered briefly what champagne McKeany would be drinking, what tailored suit he would be wearing and which beautiful woman would want to fuck the all-important anatomist of the North East, and how he liked it. Maybe McKeany preferred boys? Well, he could have who the fuck he chose. He was now *the* Doctor McKeany. Bitterness aside, Geordie knew a good partnership when he saw one. He may have been out here in the cold and dark, blood literally on his hands, sneaking around like a dock rat escaping a ship, but he was pleased with how McKeany was dealing with matters. The note was subtle and carried no names. It would have been dangerous to communicate face-to-face and payment was always ready. Anyway, Mill was a smart man. He knew men had their place in the world and his place was fucking whores any way he wanted whilst drinking ale and winning at cards. Drinking champagne from a thin flute in a ridiculous sleeved shirt – no, that certainly wasn't his bag. Good luck to McKeany. As long as he got the money, all was good. And he did. Because he knew he was *very* fucking good at this business. Possibly even the *very* best. The night was young and after losing out on that damn tobacco, Geordie decided to head out to look for another body. Two in one night was risky, but as he'd proved to himself time and time again, he, Geordie Mill, was the top man at this. He smiled his self-assured grin to no one in particular and reasoned that he could then take the rest of the week off and buy himself his own goddamn snuff.

All the snuff he wanted.

And booze.

And whores.

Geordie walked out into the cold streets of Dundee like a predator roaming his wild habitat.

*

As the rain turned from a gentle drizzle into a full-blown shower, Geordie began to question his earlier decision. The cash still sat tight in his pocket untouched, and he knew of at least four late night drinking dens he could visit at this time of night. At either one of these he could have a chat, get into a fight, win a game of cards or even fuck a whore. It was indeed time to cash in his payment and start enjoying some of the finer things Dundee had to offer. As he walked the streets, the downpour of rain did nothing to dampen the smell of whale blubber. In fact, it only amplified the stench. The rain was cold yet it revived Geordie somehow, washing the grime off the streets and making the human waste flow weaker, which did succeed in diluting its intoxicating smell. A dog ran past him, also looking for cover. Geordie thought about getting one of the mangy, flea-ridden animals as a pet. *They'd be better company than half the people of this city,* he reasoned. *And all they do is eat, sleep and fuck. God must have put me in the wrong body.*

As Geordie compared his lot with that of a canine's, a carriage stopped a little way in front of him. A gentleman jumped out from the driver's seat and opened one of the carriage doors.

Geordie wondered why the rich simply couldn't walk. Did money stop your fucking limbs from working? He watched as two ladies stepped out. They were huddled together and one of them was clutching an umbrella, attempting to shield them both from the driving rain. The driver promptly closed the carriage door and climbed back into his seat. He was obviously in a rush to get home to the comfort of his own bed.

Curious about what two young, well-to-do ladies were doing out at this time of night, Geordie crossed the cobbled street and began following them. He could hear one thanking the other for the wonderful evening and for getting her home. The other told her not to be silly, she was glad to have company. The ladies' laughter filled the streets. As Geordie was about to overtake them he realised the carriage had sped away and the rest of the street was empty. And the rain was loud. He looked around again and, feeling cheered by their lack of company, started doing some maths in his head. How long would it take for the rain to stop? How long would it take him to collect that wheelbarrow and rush back to McKeany's? How much of the ladies' screams would the rain cover? *Three* deliveries in one night. Was he getting too cocky for his own good? As these questions rattled through his mind, he thought about McKeany's success, the note he'd written and the tobacco which had cruelly escaped his enjoyment.

Hold on, he was Geordie Mill. He could do fucking *anything* he put his mind to.

He reached into his inside coat pocket, the opposite one to where his cash was snug, and removed a large wrap of cloth. Unravelling it, he took out the knife he *always* carried. He was from Lochee and this was Dundee. In his line of business it would be suicide not to carry your own weapon. Gripping the handle he looked towards the two young females sniggering in the rain. Their bodies were young, healthy and fresh. Hell,

McKeany may even pay him *double* for such good specimens. He gripped the knife tighter and took another look around the deserted street. It was time to earn some more money.

The young ladies were both facing away from Geordie and were completely oblivious to his presence. Their innocence astonished him. The woman wrestling with the umbrella was holding her right arm up straight, giving Geordie a perfect area to stab. He could dispatch her with one swift movement, in and out. Geordie decided to strangle the other one. It would be less messy, less noisy and better for these damn stupid medical students. Geordie had another quick look around before increasing his pace until he was close up behind the women. Without further ado he thrust the knife into the ribs of the one with the umbrella.

The ensuing scream was more muted than Geordie had expected. His victim crumbled to the ground like a ragdoll, whilst her umbrella fell onto her friend. As her knees buckled and she dropped ungraciously onto the wet cobbles, Geordie grabbed at the other one, putting his arms around her slender neck and squeezing it as hard as he possibly could. The sound of gargling could be vaguely heard through the rain, but soon it stopped and he felt the body go stiff. He let go and the woman hit the ground with a thud, collapsing like a sack of potatoes. Meanwhile, the other woman was still writhing around and snuffling like a sow in the dirty streets. Her hands were wrapped around her cut in a vain attempt to stem the bleeding. Geordie grabbed her long hair and pulled her up onto her knees before cutting her delicate throat. As she collapsed on the ground next to her friend, Geordie placed his hands on his knees and bent over, taking a series of deep breaths. Killing was indeed an exhausting business.

He didn't allow himself to fully regain his breath back before springing into action once again. One at a time he dragged the two women across the wet street and positioned them ungraciously in a darkened corner where they'd be out the way of any passers-by. Thunder cracked overhead and the rain continued to pour. Geordie Mill walked off swiftly to collect the wheelbarrow and some more blankets. Hopefully, the rain would wash away some of the blood from his top and the stench of whale blubber would overpower the aroma of death, which clung to his nostrils as he quickened his pace.

*

The rain was beginning to subside, as was Geordie's buoyant mood. As he pushed the empty wheelbarrow back through the streets, his shoulders and back throbbed and he felt his confidence flow away like the human waste under the wheelbarrow's three wheels as it swam through the gaps in the cobbles. *Three* bodies in one evening. Maybe he had gone *too* far this time.

Anyway, in hindsight, the one with the stab wounds and sliced neck would be no good for McKeany's work. They would know the nature of her demise and question the doctor. The other one, however, would be perfect. He wondered what to do. Leave the no-good one where she was or take them both to the shed for McKeany to figure out? He was the fucking scholar after all. Or should he throw the surplus body in the Tay? These questions were still going through Geordie's mind when he heard a slight commotion ahead. He stopped in his tracks and listened to the slightly raised tones just around the corner. Leaning his wheelbarrow against the nearest wall he walked as casually as he possibly could towards the place where he'd dumped the bodies.

Shit.

Three people were already huddled around the bodies. Geordie's first instinct was to stop in his tracks, turn around and run the fuck away. But he couldn't. This kind of behaviour would make him a suspect. The trio would see his bloody shirt, spot the wheelbarrow and then do some simple maths. Shit, shit, *shit*.

Geordie summoned all his will and continued to walk towards the three men. They were holding up their lanterns and illuminating the disregarded heap. Geordie attempted to appear normal.

"Evening, gents," he said smiling. "Dreadful weather we're having."

"Just keep on walking, sir," said a man with a thick moustache.

"Why, why what is …"

"Nothing to bother yourself with, sir. Just keep on walking and be careful out tonight. Understand?"

"Well okay, sir," said Geordie in the most innocent tone he could muster. He kept his chin low and his collar up as he did what he was told and carried on walking. They would never guess the murderer would walk back to his victims. No one was that bold. But he *had* left the wheelbarrow around the corner and now it was simply too risky to collect it. Shit, shit, *shit*.

Geordie kept on walking, cursing his own greed as the rain soaked through his clothes. It was a problem he would have to figure out on his own and in the dry. Damn it, he knew he should have found a game of cards or gotten himself into a fight. Things would have been a hell of a lot easier with a black eye and an emptier wallet.

Three of the local Dundee Police Force ran past him, lanterns swinging in their hands, urgent expressions on their faces.

At least I won't be the only poor bugger at work tonight, Geordie thought to himself.

CHAPTER XVIII

MR JOHN WILSON contemplated how the relentless rain did nothing to wash the dirt, filth and the grime from the street of the disgusting, terrible city he'd found himself in. He stared out of his window as the streets below filled with water, carrying piss, shit and leftover food along with it. He wondered if that dear old woman had given her husband his special gift yet. If so, would he be attempting to swallow his tongue or gouging out his eyes? Or would it already be all over for him? He looked from the rain battering the window to the small wooden table in front of him where there were three pouches still to go. These were the final lot. He'd decided once these were dispatched he was done with Dundee. He could do *no* more. He'd been sent to fix the problem of the city's sin, but if he was completely honest with himself, he'd barely made a dent.

He'd eradicated two whores, two gamblers and four Dundonians. He was sure these people were beyond forgiveness, beyond redemption and beyond saving, but there were hundreds more where they came from. Quite simply, Mr John Wilson, right-hand soldier to the Lord above, didn't have the resources to complete his work. He closed his eyes and silently begged for forgiveness over his failure, though he felt another flood was needed for such a vast area, not a foot soldier. As his eyes closed, his mind wandered from his conversation with the Lord to the less-than-recent past. He thought back to the time when he was 10 and had bitten into an apple as he sat on the ground outside his home. He recalled the sweet flavour as the refreshing juice filled his young mouth, the crunching sound the fruit made bringing joy as the beautiful taste lingered on his lips. It was a perfect moment - right up until he spotted the shadow of his father standing over him, dew clinging to his legs and feet. His father was a big man and the shadow he cast was even bigger. The memory was as fresh in John's mind as if it had happened only yesterday. He supposed this was only to be expected, as the memory had resurfaced on a daily basis since the event took place. Sometimes it came to him in his sleep, other times when he prayed or his thoughts were drifting a little. It served him right… drifting thoughts were sinful and he should practice better self-discipline. His father asked him where he had got the apple, which was now half-eaten and resting in the palm of his small hand. John thought of a half-truth that he hoped would suffice, but it felt as if his father's eyes were boring holes into him and this filled him with fear. He knew the truth would have to be told.

"I found it, Father," he said, looking up from the damp grass.
"Where?"

"It was on the pew next to us at church this morning."

"So you picked it up and stole it?"

"No…no, I didn't st-steal it, but I…I…pick…"

"Did it belong to you, John?"

"No, Father."

"Did you *steal it*?"

"Yes, Father."

"From God's own home?"

"Yes, Father."

"Do you think it may have been the Devil tempting you like he did in the good book, my son?"

John knew not to disagree with the man who knew everything.

"Yes, Father."

"And you, my son, gave in to temptation and carried out the Devil's plan by *stealing* something that wasn't yours?"

John Wilson looked again at the half-eaten apple, which was now beginning to turn brown. The glorious sweet taste was turning sour in his mouth.

"Yes, Father."

"Stand up, my son," said Mr Wilson, "and put the rest of the apple on the ground."

John Wilson stared out of the window as he recalled all those years spent standing in the shadow of this great man, a man who had never missed a day of worship in his life. He and his mother had looked after John and his elder brother, Allan, so well. He remembered how bad he'd felt when the realisation struck that he had let his father down with his sinful ways. The Devil had outsmarted him. He also recalled the beating that followed, how he'd tried not to cry as his father whacked him continuously with a large stick. Later on, he'd sat at the table, still in pain, tears continually falling from his itchy, puffy eyes as his father talked to Allan while completely ignoring him. His mother, a weak, thin woman with shallow blue eyes and a timid voice attempted to talk to John and bring him out of his pain, but she wasn't the person he wanted to communicate with. Who was *she* anyway? A woman his father had picked out of the gutter. It was his father he so desperately wanted to speak with. He listened as he talked to Allan about the day's sermon, and the work that needed doing around their home. John knew he was being ostracised from them, which was far worse a punishment than any beating. As he felt his back itch where the cuts were beginning to heal, he continued to ignore his mother and listen to his brother and father instead. They conversed like two brothers. His eyes remained puffy for days.

Over the next few years, John watched as Allan's body grew

bigger, his shoulders widened and his voice deepened. As his brother so obviously turned into a man, his father readily took him under his wing and the two often prayed together. Meanwhile, his own height seemed to be stunted and his shoulders never widened as much as his brother's. His face was covered in fluff whilst his brother's was covered in *hair*. His mother tried to bond with him as his father had bonded with Allan, but this offended him even more. He didn't want a *woman's* comfort.

He knew that all his pain was due to his one act of sin in taking the apple. The Devil got the better of him and he was yet to be forgiven.

As a teenager, John had sat at the table watching his weak mother boil some vegetables whilst his father and Allan were out visiting an important clergyman. At that moment, he knew he would fight on and find redemption.

Now, those days were long gone, yet John continued to pray. He decided to get some rest. After all, he had three pouches left and the Lord's work was never done.

CHAPTER XIX

GEORDIE NARROWED HIS eyes and squinted as, by some miracle, a ray of sunlight broke through the thick clouds and smog and shone over Dundee. He lay on his bed, fully clothed from the previous night, his jacket and trousers still soaked through from the torrential rain. He wiped his face with the palm of his hands and the events of last night swooped into his mind and hit him like a sledgehammer. He sat upright, feeling bile enter his mouth as he attempted to get the events in some kind of sensible order. The killing, the note, the knife, the two young ladies – *shit, what was he thinking?* The discovery, the wheelbarrow. *Shit, shit, shit. The damn wheelbarrow.*

Geordie got to his feet and pulled off his damp clothes. Dumping them on the floor, he replaced them with dry ones that at least wouldn't connect him to last night. Damn it, why had he gotten so greedy? He picked up his wet coat, removed the knife from the inside pocket and placed it underneath his bed for disposal later. *Shit.*

His boots were still wet but they were his only pair so he had no choice but to put them on. He strode off in the direction of the crime scene, *his* crime scene. He needed to know if that damn wheelbarrow had been discovered. His heart raced as he picked up his pace.

★

On his way to the scene he bought a newspaper. At least it gave him a reason to be walking around the streets. The first thing he discovered was that the bodies had been removed. Although this was no surprise, he wondered for a moment whether he had simply dreamt the whole thing up. But, as he walked around the corner, his hopes and dreams of having an overactive imagination vanished. He saw his wheelbarrow propped up exactly where he had left it the previous evening. The two bodies and the cart obviously hadn't been connected. The distance between them had so far worked in his favour. Geordie was glad. He knew that if the wheelbarrow were gone *he* would also be a goner. With the price they fetched in scrap it would seem suspect if one were left behind at the best of times. But left behind in the vicinity of two dead women would definitely be seen as suspicious. If he believed in such a figure he would have thanked God for the fact it hadn't yet been discovered. Instead, he looked around and walked towards the wheelbarrow. His mind spun. Was this a trap? Some kind of convoluted plan to catch him? Geordie knew how inefficient the Police were, but he was wary even so. He opened up the paper and, pretending to read, walked gingerly towards the cart. He counted to thirty seconds, perhaps the longest thirty seconds of his life, put the newspaper in the wheelbarrow, picked up its handles and began to push it to McKeany's.

*

Donald McNabb looked out of his window and was pleasantly surprised at the sun's valiant effort to break through to the streets of the Ferry below. Some sun was just what he needed. A little light might help him get back on track. It was a sign. He turned around and looked at his unmade bed. Since Angela had been taken by that foul illness, it had gone from their haven to a very lonely place indeed. For a year now, not a day had gone by when he hadn't questioned how a God could make such a foul thing happen to one so lovely. She was good, pretty and she said her prayers every night. But that didn't stop her flesh decaying, her body convulsing and her blood turning her handkerchief scarlet every time she coughed. The day she died in his arms was the day he knew *his* life was over too. His desire had gone and his faith had left him. But maybe this sunlight was an omen; a signal for him to get on with his clerical training and rediscover the joys of life again, instead of simply standing in his bedroom looking out of his window and observing the comings and goings of Brook Street like some sort of old, decrepit spinster. He decided he would visit Father Callahan again and discuss his future with the church. But at the moment he finally made up his mind to do this, he spotted something very suspicious indeed – a large man with a wheelbarrow was opening up the side gate and entering Paul McKeany's backyard. He placed the wheelbarrow against the outhouse and exited through the same side entrance. He did this without knocking on the door, or looking up. In fact, he was in and out like a thief in the night. McNabb decided that this was very suspicious behaviour indeed. What was McKeany's profession again? He couldn't recall, but maybe he would ask Betty Cleary next door. She was the oracle of neighbourhood gossip. Yes, that's what he would do. McNabb left his window and got dressed as the sun continued to fight through the Dundee smog.

★

Geordie Mill walked through his front door, dumped himself on his wooden chair next to his slightly unbalanced wooden table and immediately placed his head in his hands. He had been too greedy, too careless, too reckless, and yet his luck had somehow managed to stay intact. Next time he wouldn't be so gung-ho. He took another deep breath and relaxed his shoulders. This should be a day for enjoying himself, not thinking about work, bodies and barrows. He leant back, placed his boots on the table and began to read his paper. The third page grabbed his undivided attention. His boots slid back to the floor as he shuffled forwards to be closer to the print.

The *Edinburgh Evening Courant* yesterday indicated strongly that the city may be closer to solving a certain series that has haunted it for many a year. An old woman of the name Campbell, from Ireland, came to Edinburgh and took up lodgings on Friday, in the house of a man named Burt or Burke, in the West Port. It appears there was a merry making in Burke's that night. The old woman, it is said, with reluctance joined in the mirth, and also partook of the liquor. During the night shrieks were heard; but the neighbours paid no attention, as such sounds were not unusual in the house. In the morning, however, a female, on going into Burke's, observed the old woman lying as if dead, some of the straw being above her. After a search, the body was found yesterday morning in the lecture room of a respectable practitioner, who, the instant he was informed of the circumstance, not only gave it up, but afforded every information in his power. The body is now in the police office, and will be examined by medical gentlemen in the course of the day. There are some very strong and singular circumstances connected with the case, which have given rise to suspicions.

Geordie Mill reread the article once more. William Burke's number was up. The last time he'd heard from his old pal from Edinburgh was when he'd shared a safe house with him, Hare, Greg and Jamie. Damn it. It looked like the authorities were edging closer to his game too. Damn it to hell. Well, at least he'd gotten away with the killings last night. Maybe he should keep his head down for a day or two. Yes, it was time to put business on hold before lady luck gave up, showed her cards and went home.

CHAPTER XX

THE SUN MAY have gone on to hide under the city's smog, but Donald McNabb's attitude seemed a little lighter. He removed his outdoor jacket and hat and placed them on his bed. The meeting with Father Callahan had definitely been worth it. They had discussed faith and the need to keep busy, even in the face of loss. They shared bread and Father Callahan showed Donald his small garden at the back of the churchyard. He beamed with pride while pointing out the small flowers that were growing despite Dundee's industrial activities and the pollution they generated. Father Callahan had set out to inspire Donald and he'd achieved his aim. He'd vowed to tidy himself up, take a walk and possibly buy himself something to eat and drink.

"A decent meal will do both your constitution and your mind wonders," Father Callahan told him.

Choosing a clean shirt to wear, Donald took another look out of his window. His talk with Father Callahan was temporarily forgotten. Two members of the Dundee Police Force were standing outside Dr McKeany's front door. They were clutching their lamps tightly and their batons were swinging at their sides. Donald continued to watch as one of them knocked on his front door. *Was it anything to do with that gentleman taking an empty wheelbarrow and placing it against the outhouse?* From his high position, Donald could see the wheelbarrow still propped up against it. Maybe he should quickly put on his shirt and jacket and inform them what he had seen. Possibly Dr McKeany had reported it missing and was now going to make a fool of himself, as it had been there all along. But why would the police make such a fuss over a missing piece of gardening equipment? McNabb thought it unlikely it would command such attention, what with the recent spate in burking. He dwelled on it some more as he continued to stare at the goings on below him, his shirt half off and half on.

Dr McKeany came to the front door. It looked like he was asking the policeman a question, but McNabb couldn't be so sure from his position at the window. Just then, Dr McKeany fell to the ground and started howling like a dog. The two policeman grabbed him gently by the arms and took him into his home, closing the door behind them.

Something is very strange indeed, Donald McNabb concluded as he finally got his shirt on and put on his hat.

⋆

Craig Boyd's feet throbbed as he walked the streets of the Ferry with his once optimistic partner, Graham Whyte. The blisters on both his feet were due for a popping and his legs felt like someone had injected them with lead piping, but he was done moaning about his physical ailments. Likewise, Whyte was done with listening to him moan about them. Both Craig and Graham knew each other's tolerance levels, and both had reached their threshold. So they kept quiet about their ailments and talked of other things instead. The main topic of conversation was their stupidity about the glamour involved in being part of Dundee's Police Force. They'd harboured thoughts of chivalry and heroism, thought they would be bought drinks by the men and be spoilt for choice when it came to the woman. Huh. Instead there'd been nothing but blisters, dirty looks, jibes in the street, people spitting in their general direction and the constant noise of people tutting at them. The Police Force as a career move had been a bad one. And now, well hell, it was about to get *worse*.

They walked in silence towards the home of Dr McKeany. They were both dreading the job ahead. They had been sold down the river, that was for sure, and today's instruction was not worth all the money in the world. They continued to walk down the road until they reached the large house where the rising star of the medical world and, according to the authorities and press, all round nice guy, lived.

Graham and Craig each took a deep breath and composed themselves. And, as Craig knocked three times on the door, they glanced at each other, both sharing a defeated outlook. The door took a while to open and, to their shame, both police officers immediately wished it hadn't.

They were met with quite a sight. McKeany was unshaven, his hair was unkempt and his eyes were as wide as saucers. Yesterday the press had displayed a picture of Dr McKeany in all his glory. He was wearing his best suit and a sparkle was evident in his eyes. It was astonishing what difference a day could make.

"Did you find her? *Please* say you've found her, gentlemen? I mean, she was having a great time last night but she assured me she wanted to get her dear cousin home. Oh dear, I got home and waited and waited. Then when I spoke to you gentlemen this morning, I was *assured* you would do all you could. Oh gentlemen, *please* say you've found my dear Charlotte."

McKeany tugged Craig's elbow as he spoke, before grabbing his arm. Craig slowly shook his limb free, glanced at Graham and then looked again at the desperate, broken man in front of him. It was plain he had attempted to sleep, but he hadn't changed out of last night's clothes. His white shirt and black

157

dining suit were crumpled where he must have lain down in them.

"Doctor McKeany, if you could come down the station with us," Graham Whyte said in quiet voice. "It may not be best to discuss matters here."

Graham kept his eyes fixed on the doctor's tear-filled, saucer-shaped eyes. No more words had to be said. Doctor Paul McKeany, the man of the hour, fell on his knees and sobbed into his hands like an infant in need of his mother.

CHAPTER XXI

THE TWO WATCHMEN, Robin Andrews and Scott Long, stood as quiet as they could and listened to one of the Howff Cemetery's tall doors creak. Dundee was on high alert and the Charlies, unfortunately, were directly in the firing line. The general public were linking the gruesome murder of the anatomist's wife and the spate of people being poisoned with the incidents of grave robbing, and tensions around all the local burial grounds were high. Two of the lads on shift last month had been attacked, which meant the two watchmen couldn't relax, even just for a minute. Emotions, the Charlies had realised, had no logic. So when they heard the door creak they remained as still as the night itself. At this late hour on a Saturday night, they knew no one had lawful business for being in the cemetery. They crept forward, clutching the handle of their recently assigned pistols in one hand and holding their lanterns aloft in the other. The body of Jean Anderson, a young lady who had succumbed to whooping cough, had been laid to rest the previous day and the watchmen had been given strict instruction the body should remain where it belonged, no matter what. And, after the unprovoked incident last month at the Logie, both men were determined to do the right thing.

Ten or so seconds went by, then another 10. Just as they began to calm down they heard a whistle from one edge of the Howff and an instant reply from the other. Then silence.

"Who's there?" Robin, the taller of the two watchmen, shouted. "We're armed and we *will* shoot anyone who comes near the graves!"

There was no reply. Both men stayed stationary for a further six or seven minutes. Again, just as they dared to move, the sound of another whistle could be heard, followed by another. Shooting a look at one another, both men fired their pistols in the air. The orange spark illuminated the dark cemetery, the roar of the shots echoed through the night sky. The result was immediate. There was the sound of people running and the creak of the door as the potential grave robbers made their speedy retreat.

*

Donald McNabb had a purpose. Father Callahan had been right, he'd just needed a focal point, a reason to live. And this little mystery may yet prove to be such a distraction. Watching McKeany crumble to his knees outside his own home filled Donald with sadness. He was still standing at the window five minutes later when he and the two police officers came out of the house. Tears were still visible on McKeany's pale face and his shoulders were rising up and down like those of a hysterical child. McNabb wondered what had happened and where his young wife was. Above all, he wondered who the large man was and what he'd been doing with McKeany's wheelbarrow. He had recognised him and was sure he was a local. He didn't think it would be that hard for him find out his name.

*

As Robin and Scott began their ten o'clock Sunday shift, they realised the resurrectionists had started their work slightly earlier. After the previous evening, they were anxious but on full alert. As their lanterns swung from their waist, it was Scott who fell into the gaping hole where the grave of Jean Anderson should have been. With a shriek he fell onto his arse, his lantern projecting a widening arc of light.

"Shit!" he shouted, desperately trying to gain his bearings and clamber out of the freshly-dug hole.

"STOP THERE!" Robin shouted in no particular direction. "We *will* shoot!"

He noticed two men walking slowly towards him. One was pulling a sack, the other was holding the handle of a spade, which was dragging along the earth.

"DO NOT MOVE!" Robin shouted, pointing his pistol at the two men.

Scott was still attempting to leverage himself up with his hands, but the earth was crumbling between his fingers.

As the pistol wavered in his hand, the two men stopped ten yards away.

"We'll do you a deal," the man holding the spade said. "You let us take the body and I *promise* you we'll give you a slice of the pie."

"GET YOUR HANDS IN THE AIR OR WE WILL SHOOT," shouted Robin. Meanwhile, Scott was still battling with the hole, which was well on its way to claiming victory.

The two grave robbers walked slowly towards the watch-men.

"We'll give you *half*. You can't say fairer than that."

"I said..." but before Robin could complete his warning, the resurrectionist with the spade swung it at him. He missed and Robin stumbled backwards into Scott, who had just managed to regain his balance and clamber onto higher ground. He promptly fell back into the ditch, but this time with Robin. As they were falling, Robin took aim but cursed as the primer from his firing pan fell out. Scrambling over his partner, he reloaded the pistol but the two grave robbers were already retreating through the gravestones. They were long gone by the time Robin fired.

The watchmen gradually regained their composure and ungraciously clambered out of the ditch. They walked towards where the resurrectionsts had attempted to strike a deal. It was there that Scott stumbled over one disregarded spade and the freshly dug-up body of Jean Anderson.

*

"Hey, Geordie. Stupid question I ken, but by any chance were you pushing a wheelbarrow doon the Ferry yesterday?"

Geordie Mill looked up at the landlord, his mouth open like a hooked fish. "Eh?"

The large, ruddy-faced landlord repeated himself whilst wiping the bar with a towel that was obviously only being kept together by dirt. "Were you pushing a wheelbarrow doon the Ferry yesterday?"

It gave Geordie a little time to compose himself. "No. Why do you ask?"

"It's just some guy was asking earlier on today, when I was doon the butchers. His description was pretty accurate y'ken."

"Who?" Geordie said, taking a sip from his ale if only to hide a little of his face. His heart felt like it was going to beat itself out of his thick chest.

"Don't ken," replied the landlord. "Nice chap. Friendly like. Grey hair. Thick red eyebrows, a kind of baby face. Donald maybe, can't really remember, Geordie."

"Did you say it may have been me you saw? I mean, it wasn't y'ken, but just wondering."

Shit, shit, shit.

"Nah," replied the landlord. Geordie nearly leant over and kissed the ruddy-faced man. "I just heard him talking. Never got involved."

"Oh well, it wasn't me anyhow. Nae bother," Geordie said as he went to sit at his usual table, where Greg and Jamie were already seated. His mind was now filled with thoughts and doubts. Shit. *Who the fuck saw me with that wheelbarrow and why is he asking the fuck around? Shit, shit, shit.*

He managed to plaster a grin on his face so as not to reveal anything to the younger men. He thought of the knife under his bed and the two girls piled on top of each other. His heart wouldn't stop racing.

"You okay there, Geordie?" Greg enquired. "You look like you've seen a ghost."

Geordie didn't reply. He didn't even threaten Greg with violence. His palms were open, not even forming a fist. Something, Greg realised, was definitely not quite right.

He and Jamie continued to drink their ales whilst Geordie sat in silence. Just as they were about to finish their tankards, two men ran into the tavern and started a commotion.

"Shots have been heard oot in the Howff!" one of them shouted.

Half the tavern's patrons immediately rose to their feet and headed towards the burial ground.

"They must have got the bastards!"

"Kill 'em!"

"Bury 'em alive!"

Geordie, Jamie and Greg leapt to their feet and joined the crowd, following them across the road and into the large, open doors of the Howff. Within the space of three minutes, a crowd of 20 had convened from the local alehouses. They were joined by people from the surrounding houses. Geordie noted how they were mainly angry women. The crowd soon gained momentum, but it quickly become clear that the culprits had already made their escape.

The two watchmen, who were still brandishing their pistols, were bombarded with questions and accusations. Robin recalled the incident with the Charlies up at the Logie and quickly launched his defence.

"They had guns, too!" he said. "But we managed to get back the girl."

But it was the sight of Jean Anderson, her glazed eyes open as she lay half in and half out of the sack that stirred the anger of the crowd even more. Thankfully for Scott and Robin, this wasn't aimed at then. It was acknowledged they had at least prevented a crime from taking place. Geordie walked through the mob listening to people blaming the police, the anatomists and the Charlies.

"There was a couple here from Edinburgh. I betcha it was them. I saw them today doon the Overgate."

"Aye, me too. They looked shifty as hell."

"Aye."

Throughout the chaos, the baying crowd slowly departed, walking off in dribs and drabs while still mumbling about the burkers and the state of society. They were clutching spades, pitchforks, steel bars, pieces of iron railings, rolling pins and knives and they were on the hunt for *anyone* they could blame.

Geordie wondered how many innocent people would be beaten or stabbed as the mob desperately tried to vent their frustrations. He also wondered who was worse. At least the gravediggers had a purpose for their violence. But it barely mattered to him. The baying crowd, the mistake he'd made by bludgeoning the two women, the mutterings of the landlord in the pub and the hanging of his pal Hare in Edinburgh had made him decide it was time to call it a day. He'd get his final payment from McKeany and head west, or even south over the border.

As Geordie reached this momentous decision, the moon decided to appear from the behind the clouds, illuminating the face of a man stood nearby. He was going round asking people questions. He also seemed to be looking in Geordie's direction.

As the crowd departed, Greg and Jamie nudged their boss's arm.

"Nothing to see here, Geordie," said Greg, his cheeks wobbling. "Let's get back to our drinks, eh? Before some wee bastard steals 'em, like."

"Aye," replied Geordie and looked back at Greg. By the time he looked away again the man asking questions was lost in the crowd. Geordie was sure he was the one who'd been in the pub enquiring about the wheelbarrow. He had the grey hair, the baby face and the thick red eyebrows the landlord had described.

Perhaps one more body for the anatomist wasn't a bad idea after all, Geordie decided.

PART THREE

CHAPTER 1

"**H**USH HUSH NOW," Dr Fairborough said gently, reaching an arm awkwardly around his sobbing son-in-law's shoulder. "Don't cry."

He possessed civility and intelligence in abundance, but emotional support wasn't something that came easy to him. It wasn't as if he lacked feeling, though. In fact, tears had been silently falling down his own cheeks for two hours as the two men sat in the cold back room of the town hall, which had been turned into a temporary morgue. However, a lifetime of displaying his good breeding prevented a howl, yowl or shake. For him, there'd be no panting, screaming or shouting. There'd be no hysterics, though he hadn't been able to avoid shedding tears over the death of his beautiful young daughter. She was his only daughter and he'd brought her up so well, helped her turn into a sophisticated, intelligent and modest young woman.

Paul McKeany sat slouched next to him, snot escaping from his nostrils and a string of drool hanging from his bottom lip. With his superior knowledge of the human body and familiarity with corpses, the superintendant of Dundee Police Force wrongly assumed he'd be less affected by the task of identifying his wife.

But, when McKeany walked into the cold room and a thin, balding police officer pulled down a cloth to expose Charlotte's once beautiful face, McKeany had clocked her blackened eyes and agonising final posture and fallen to his knees again and wailed like a rabid dog. The police officer promptly covered the face up again and required no further confirmation. Eventually, McKeany clambered back onto his feet via his knees and another police officer led him back to the waiting area where his father-in-law was seated.

Dr Fairborough didn't feel the need to say goodbye to his daughter. He would wait until the burial. McKeany's face had told him all he needed to know. No good would come out of him also confirming that the sliced-up mess on the mortuary slab was his baby girl.

The police officer left the two grown men alone with their grief. They sat together on a wooden bench looking at the ground below and sniffing into their sodden handkerchiefs. It was such a terrible and cruel loss.

An hour had passed by the time Graham Whyte and Craig Boyd entered the town hall and were directed to the waiting room. As the two men walked into the room, Dr Fairborough stood up before reaching out to shake their hands. Graham had to admire his professionalism in a time like this. He knew he wouldn't be so courteous if the tables were turned. Meanwhile, he wasn't even sure if Dr McKeany had noticed them arrive. He was slouched over with his head firmly in his hands. Broken was a term that came to mind.

"Dr Fairborough, Doctor McKeany," Graham said. "Sorry for the delay, but we...we have procedures to go through."

"Of course, of course," Dr Fairborough replied.

McKeany's head never left his hands, but both officers were aware of his shuddering shoulders rising up and down. They wondered if the sobbing would ever cease.

Craig decided to take over. "We are, of course, investigating who in the world would carry out such an act, and all avenues need to be investigated. So, if you would kindly accompany us, we would like to do a quick check of your home, Doctor McKeany, and the surroundings, of course. You know, in case we find…"

"NO!"

McKeany had stood up in a flash, causing all three of the room's other occupants to jump.

"Paul?" Dr Fairborough said, getting to his feet a tad slower than his son-in-law. "It's only a procedure…for clues, you know."

Graham and Craig both noted that McKeany had gone from a mild-mannered professional to a wild animal in the space of 24 hours. Drool stuck to his chin and snot covered his left nostril. His eyes were red raw and puffy and his cheeks were gaunt. Both Graham and Craig also noted that he looked…scared.

"We need to let them do anything they can to find out *who* did this to our Charlotte," Dr Fairborough said.

McKeany's shoulders dropped and his head slumped down once again. His eyes seemed to shrink into their sockets and his chin, if at all possible, dropped down even further. He thought of his garden, the wheelbarrow, the outhouse and the bodies inside it. He'd be known as the murdering doctor whose wife was killed the same way his victims were. No, that wasn't fair, but he knew how people's minds worked. They wouldn't understand that his motives had been good ones, how he'd simply wanted to help his students get a better understanding of the human body. They would simply just see *the* bodies. Paul McKeany realised he was a dead man walking.

"Paul, you understand that…"

Paul held his hands up, palms facing upwards, and looked into his father-in-law's bloodshot blue eyes. This was his hero, his idol.

"Yes, I understand. Lead the way, gentlemen."

The four men left the town hall and headed to a waiting carriage, which would take them back to Brooke Street. If anyone happened to look out of the window it may have appeared that one of them was walking towards a hangman's noose.

CHAPTER II

THE OLD MAN stopped walking and stood dead in his tracks. He stood as still as a statue. The night had been very similar to the last two or three. Perhaps it had been *too* familiar. A few ales in The John O'Groats at Cowgate followed by a walk home past the Wishart Memorial Church. The locals called The John O'Groats Heaven and Hell and William Paul understood why. The ales flowed, as did the company, but occasionally the ales didn't flow enough and the company got tetchy. Tetchiness soon turned to anger, anger soon transformed to full-on violence. Fistfights were common in the tavern, but there were never any really serious felonies.

Anyway, William always minded his own business. He was way too old and wise to share his opinion. That meant he never got into any arguments. If only he had done that when he was younger. Anyway, that evening had been no different to any other in the week. He'd drank Indian pale ale and watched some ladies of the night desperately looking for business. A small, hairy Greek man had lost an arm wrestle to a well-endowed Lochee woman who sported stray hairs on her chin and a large boil on her nose.

About ten minutes after he left the pub, William Paul saw his life flash in front of his eyes. A pedestrian had walked right into him outside the tavern and their shoulders had clashed, leaving William gasping for air. Instead of the usual aggravation he assumed would follow, the man he'd collided with simply picked up the pouch of tobacco he'd dropped, stood up straight and apologised.

"I'm so sorry, sir," he said, offering him the pouch, "please take this by way of an apology".

The stranger walked away before William could refuse the kind gift. He immediately unravelled the pouch, allowing the beautiful smell of dry tobacco to caress his nostrils. What a piece of luck! Just then, William Paul's memory triggered into action and saved his life. He recalled a recent chat in the John O'Groats. The two lads sitting next to him - police officers perhaps - were moaning about their lot when their conversation had taken a strange turn, causing William's ears to prick up. They started chatting about five, six or maybe seven murders where all the victims had been horrifically poisoned. And *yes* – they thought the poison was hidden in *tobacco*. Shit, that was definitely it – tobacco! And *why* in God's name would someone just give him a pouch of tobacco? His body froze solid as he realised what he was holding. Possibly it was all a coincidence. Perhaps this gentleman *was* what he appeared to be - a kind and generous stranger. *But this is Dundee*, William mused. He wondered what he should do. The local Charlies would have enough on their hands and the town hall was more than a mile away. William Paul snapped out of his trance and decided to follow the gift supplier. He hadn't exactly been a spring chicken, so he couldn't have gotten far.

William placed the pouch carefully in his pocket and followed Mr John Wilson to his home. That way he could give the local authorities an exact address. He hadn't felt that much purpose in life for about 20 years.

★

"You look better, Donald, more at peace with the world and yourself, if I may say so. Have you found yourself back on the road?"

Donald McNabb looked up from where he was seated on the front pew. He was always soothed by Father Callahan's soft, Irish lilt. He shuffled along the wooden bench as the grey-haired, smooth-faced priest lit the candles at the front of the church. Donald was always surprised that none went out as he glided past them. His soft touch was evident in all his movements.

"I am, Father. I am indeed," he replied. "I think the worst of it is behind me. Praise God."

"Praise God," Father Callahan repeated as he walked over to the row of pews where Donald was seated. He sat down next to him and admired his handiwork as the candles flickered. Donald watched the light reflect off the building's stained glass windows and wondered where he would be if this place of calm sanctuary didn't exist. Both men remained seated in silence for a further three or four minutes. They were deep in contemplation.

Father Callahan kept his palms flat on his knees and Donald held the Bible in front of him, though his eyes were nearly closed.

Just then, the large wooden door opened and a loud creak filled the room.

Donald remained where he was while Father Callahan stood up to welcome his visitor. His fluid movements were that of a man 20 years younger.

He was proud to be able to welcome people into the house of God. He believed it was one of his most important responsibilities and he never failed to do it with pride and enthusiasm.

"Good afternoon," he said to the large man, extending out his right hand. "Welcome and please take a seat."

The visitor took his hand and shook it before looking around and resting his gaze on Donald McNabb. Father Callahan released his hand as he saw the larger man's eyes narrow and his lips begin to pinch. Then the stranger simply turned around and walked back through the large wooden door, closing it firmly behind him and causing an echo to reverberate through the silence.

"Well, someone obviously didn't feel the need to take prayer today," Father Callahan said to Donald, the slight croak in his voice giving away his unease. The larger man had intimidated him slightly, but he shrugged his shoulders, smiled and retook his position among the pews.

But Donald McNabb wasn't smiling. In fact, his eyes had widened and his hand gripped the Bible even tighter than before. He'd recognised the looming figure of Geordie Mill straight away. And, above all, Geordie Mill had made it perfectly clear that he had recognised Donald McNabb.

The road to salvation may take a longer route after all, he thought as he began to silently pray.

*

Satisfied that the nosy bugger McNabb was the man he'd been looking for, Geordie's mind was once again filled with devious thoughts. The hustle and bustle of Dundee, the rancid aroma of boiling blubber and the clanging of metal on metal seemed to feed this state of mind. Just a week ago, Geordie had money in his pocket, no one to pilfer his takings and a hell of an earner in hand. Now things had gone to shite and he didn't know why. The two girls were a mistake, he knew that now, but when he had walked past McKeany's home to find that no one appeared to be in, he knew things were amiss. What if the bastard had moved house without telling him? Burke and Hare had been caught in Edinburgh and this had made big news. The last thing

McKeany needed was anything to connect him with those two crazy bastards. And now McNabb had spotted Geordie with McKeany's damn barrow and gotten himself involved in activities that shouldn't concern him. Geordie had watched him from afar for an hour or so and seen him entering the church. He'd shown his face inside in an attempt to scare him off, but upon seeing what a weak, wet fellow he was, well, Geordie wanted more. No, he *needed* more. If this McNabb was dealt with maybe, just maybe, things would sort themselves out. Was he the fly in the ointment? The spanner in the works? He *must* be. Anyway, there was nothing to be done regarding the doctor, *but* he could do something about McNabb. Besides, at this stage he had nothing left to lose. Thoughts of strangulation entered his mind. He saw that puny, silly face cry while he crushed those nosy, beady eyes into dust. And if McKeany was back, well, that would be the perfect ironic ending for McNabb. He saw him displayed on a table while a bunch of academics clapped and cheered at the sight of his weak heart on display. Geordie thought about Donald McNabb sitting helpless inside the church and smiled to himself. He'd put that interfering fishwife's faith to the *real* test.

"Get him! Over there. I can see him!"

"Murdering scum. Run! Hurry!"

Geordie stopped in his tracks, his murderous thoughts vanishing as the shouts behind him gained volume. His brain couldn't work fast enough, couldn't register what has happening. How *did* they know? Did that bastard McNabb give evidence *then* stow himself away in the church? Was there a fucking *mind reader* on the force now?

He wanted to look behind him but didn't dare.

"Make sure he doesn't get away!"

Within a second of the shouts, Geordie couldn't hold his patience any longer and looked over his right shoulder as three of Dundee's law enforcement officers, pistols in hand, ran directly towards him.

He froze as they approached, their faces red with anger and their eyes wide with determination. Time seemed to stand still as the trio ran towards and then *around* him, one clashing shoulders with him as he sped past. Geordie continued to stare as they ran on in front, determined to get somewhere, which, he was relieved to note, obviously had nothing to do with him. Shit, he was getting scared at the tiniest of things lately. McNabb had a lot to bloody answer for - that was for sure. He regained his composure and decided to see what the fuss was about, running off in the direction of the three officers.

CHAPTER III

B Y STUFFING HIS clothes into his bag without giving them the proper care and respect they deserved, Mr Wilson was aware that he was breaking his own rules of neatness and precision. But he assumed God would understand. He heard the commotion from outside as he packed two pouches of his special tobacco.

Looking out of his window, he saw three policemen point up at him. Pistols in hand, they ran towards the building's front door. It was obvious they were readying to make an arrest.

John Wilson did not know or care how the police had caught up with him. He just knew that in order to continue with the Lord's work he needed to get out of the building. *Now.*

As he picked up his bag, one of the tobacco pouches rolled out onto the floor. Damn it all. He had no time to retrieve it as the police officers were already at his door, their loud voices bellowing. He had nowhere to run to without running into them. Gripping hold of his bag, he crouched underneath the wooden table, hoping it would give him a second more to play with. He used the extra time to ask his Lord for some much-needed help.

The front door of his home cracked and swung open, splinters filling the air as the three police officers piled in. At this moment, John Wilson spied his chance of escape. There was only one body directly between him and the remains of the swinging door. John had only one advantage – to use the element of surprise, which had always been a great friend of his. Clutching his bag tightly between his tense fingers, he rammed into the police officer who promptly fell to the ground, his pistol flying from his hand. Wilson was aware of a growing presence outside. People were leaving their homes to see what the commotion was all about. He wondered if he could use this to his advantage and mix in with the masses. He was sure they would be on his side. He knew of the force's reputation with the common people and intended to play it. But, just as this thought came to him, one of the other policeman shouted from the house, "GET HIM. WE HAVE THE SNUFF KILLER!"

Angry now, the crowd attempted to grab John as he ran past. He felt his collar being wrenched, someone pulling his shoulders, someone else kicking the bag out of his hand. By the time the fallen officer had regained his footing and his two companions had joined him outside, the baying crowd could be heard as well as seen as they aimed kicks and punches at the criminal in their midst.

The citizens of Dundee finally had a target, an outlet for all their pent-up anxiety over the city's growing crime rate. The police didn't rush to arrest their criminal. After all, it was only fair to serve the lions their share of the meat.

*

They say nothing draws a crowd like a crowd, but that isn't strictly true. Nothing draws a crowd like an *angry* crowd. As the police attempted to get the battered and bruised serial killer onto his feet, they continued with their bating. Spit and swearwords were thrown around as fists went flying. The punches were aimed at the villain, but some of them struck the two officers who were holding him down, more for his own protection than to restrain him. The violence soon stopped but the crowd didn't immediately dissipate. They wanted to watch the man who had killed many being taken to the goal. They needed to confirm it with their own eyes. They talked between themselves, their pent-up anger and frustration flowing freely as they spoke of a public hanging, of seeing justice served. Geordie wondered if they were at all aware of their double standards. Amid the chaotic scenes around him, he found himself walking into the house and entering the criminal's lodgings. He wondered if it would be like this for him if he got caught. Would he get a public beating *then* see the noose? He felt a great desire to sit and rest, even for a minute or two. He slumped down on the wooden chair next to the table. The cacophony of noise outside was slowing down a little. His head swam with images of the two dead girls and of that bastard McNabb watching him pushing the wheelbarrow. Then he saw the mob giving that old man a kicking, mashing him to death as if the two officers weren't there. But it wasn't the gentlemen they were kicking - it was him - and the mob was led by McNabb and Rosie. What the fuck was she doing? There was too much noise. But this time it wasn't outside, it was inside his own head. Opening up his hands, he dropped his head into them. If he knew how, he may have cried. But he hadn't shed a single tear since he was a baby. It was then that Geordie opened his eyes and spotted the pouch of tobacco lying disregarded on the floor between the gaps in his large fingers.

"The snuff killer?" he said quietly to himself. He attempted to focus, clearing his chaotic mind and concentrating on what the newspapers had been reporting and what the tongues wagging in the taverns had been saying. A man had been offering snuff to strangers and poisoning them horrifically. Yes, that was it. He looked at the pouch again. If things were as bad as he thought they were, if his number was indeed up, surely this would be a better way to go than by the hands of the angry mob outside. Geordie Mill quickly bent over and grabbed the pouch from the floor, pushing it securely into his trouser pocket. He stood up swiftly and walked through the battered door and past the mob. He silently gave a nod of thanks to the man who was being dragged into a carriage, the blood still flowing from his face, hands and now toothless mouth. He headed home feeling, if anything, a little more at peace with the world.

CHAPTER IV

THE SOUNDS OF shuffling shoes and sniffles trailed by the odd sob followed them around the house. If Graham Whyte was perfectly honest, he didn't have a clue what he was meant to be looking for. Neither, he assumed, did his partner, Craig Boyd, but they had to at least *look* professional. Both police officers looked under cushions and opened drawers and wardrobes before closing them again. Meanwhile, Dr Fairborough and Dr Paul McKeany plodded slowly behind them like two scolded children.

"Right," Graham said, more to stop the sound of constant sniffling. "So, are you sure no one had an agenda against you? Can you think of any particular enemies you may have?"

"Officer," Fairborough replied, his voice as authoritative as his posture, "you don't become as successful as my son-in-law without…"

McKeany intervened, his voice full of complete resignation. "No officer. None at all."

"Well, okay," said Graham, opening and closing another cabinet, without even pretending to look this time. "Let's head outside. You have an outhouse in the garden, don't you? We could do a quick search…Dr McKeany, are you okay?"

He realised as soon as he said it what a silly question it was. Of course he *wasn't*. His wife had just been found slaughtered. But right at this second, he looked particularly pale. Like he had seen a ghost.

"Dr McKeany?"

He had stopped dead and his mouth was opening and closing like a goldfish in a bowl. Fresh tears formed from his red eyes and flowed down his cheeks into his sniffling mouth.

"Doctor McKeany, would you like a *seat*?"

His mouth opened and closed once more, then a small, odd smile formed on his lips. "No, no, let's go outside," he said.

Graham knew many a homeless man, many a drunk, a few prostitutes and a one-armed beggar. Yet he had never seen such a look of defeat in his entire life.

*

The four men walked past the wheelbarrow that was leaning against the wall of the outhouse. Graham swore he saw McKeany shiver slightly. He was walking in front of his father-in-law, his shoulders as low as any scarecrow.

"Have you got a key, Dr McKeany?" Craig asked as he fiddled with the lock. The question remained unanswered and Craig couldn't tell whether McKeany had even heard him.

Anyway, he thought, *the doctor won't be needing this shed for a while.*

"Step back, gentlemen," he said, using the front of his boot to kick the bottom of the door. The lock fell off with a jingle, making McKeany jump and produce a yelp. As the door swung open, all four men slowly walked inside.

The smell of rotten meat invaded their nostrils as they entered the threshold.

"Jesus Christ!" Exclaimed Graham as Craig covered his mouth and nose with his sleeve. "Did something *die* in here?"

Whether it was simply a figure of speech or a question, Paul McKeany didn't reply.

This was it. This was where it all ended.

He knew this as well as he knew the sky wouldn't fall, but he simply didn't care. He would never work again, not now, not ever. But soon, any second now, they would find the bodies, questions would be asked and backup would be called. McKeany decided there and then to tell the truth. They would all hear the sound of his neck snapping. Doctor Fairborough would be disgusted, of course, and his hanging would draw crowds of hundreds. The only thing that really concerned him, though, was the possibility of missing Charlotte's funeral. He closed his eyes tight and readied himself to face the music. It was inevitable, he supposed. Some people were born for success, others were born to die trying. It didn't take a genius to realise which camp he was in. Another tear squeezed from his eyelid and fell into his mouth as an image of his students dissecting his own naked body came to mind.

"God O' mighty, it stinks in here. I've seen enough. Do you use this shed, Dr McKeany?"

McKeany looked up as both police officers backed up, their arms still across their noses and partially blocking their view.

"Eh…no, not for ages," he mumbled, "years perhaps."

"Nothing there," Graham said as they all exited the shed, closing the door behind them. "I'm sorry, Dr McKeany, but somebody must have defecated in there at some point. Bloody tramps. When things clear up you may want to get that checked out. Okay, well, will you be okay here at home? Of course, we'll keep you updated on the enquiry and may need you to come back and have a word with the superintendent."

"He can stay at my house. Mrs Fairborough will make sure he's comfortable," Dr Fairborough replied, placing his hand gently on his son-in-law's back as they walked back to the main house.

When the officers left, McKeany experienced no sense of relief. Instead he felt hollow, defeated and achingly tired. He had somehow, without even trying, managed some great escape. He was back to being a victim while he was sure he should now be considered the criminal. He took a deep breath and fell into the armchair. His father-in-law went into the kitchen to make them both a cup of tea. He still wished the earth would open up and swallow him whole, but he was thankful he still had friends. His neck may *not* be snapped after all.

Extract from the *Edinburgh Evening Courant* newspaper:

Although a day of torrential rain, up to 25,000 people showed up to watch the murderer William Burke hang at 8.15 in the morning. Window seats in tenements over-looking the scaffold were hired, pricing from five shillings to one pound. However, it is unlikely that the 67-year-old French sculptress Madame Tussaud was there. She was seen boarding a boat the day after she attended the 24-hour court case which determined Burke's guilt of the murder of Mary Paterton, James Wilson and Mrs Docherty. Nelly McDougal, who had left court being found not guilty of the murder of Mrs Docherty, was also not in the crowd and has alas departed. Reports indicate she has been violently attacked by an angry mob in Perthshire. A further statement from Burke, the 36-year-old Irish man from Orrey, county Tyrone, who served seven years in the army, has now been released which has been authorised by Rev William

Reid, a Catholic priest, as well as a further three officials. The statement from the murderer who left his wife and children in Ireland claims that neither he or Hare, so far as he knows, ever were concerned in supplying any subjects for dissection except those before mentioned; and, in particular, never did so by raising dead bodies from the grave. He also declared that Doctor Knox never encouraged him, neither taught him to murder any person."

CHAPTER V

THE EAGLE INN was particularly busy today. The deformed barmaid slammed Geordie's drink down against the wooden table, but no one seemed to notice or care. Both Donald McGregor and James Jeffrey stole nervous glances at each other. Geordie hadn't cursed them or threatened them with violence once. In fact, he hadn't said much at all. This was turning into an uncomfortable ritual. If Greg and Jamie hadn't known any better, they would have thought Geordie Mill was considering his place in the world. Thinking even. Contemplating life.

Perhaps reading about his pals in Edinburgh, one in the gaol and one in the noose, had settled his nature, calmed him down and forced him to reconsider his wily ways. But they knew Geordie and so they knew that simply couldn't be true. They took another sip of their drinks, glanced at each other once more and attempted to strike up another conversation.

"Hey, Geordie. Did you hear about the snuff killer? He was caught red-handed, apparently. Just up the road as well. Maybe the police force isn't as fucking useless as we thought they were. Eh, Geordie?"

"Eh? Aye, Greg," Geordie mumbled half-heartedly whilst taking another sip of his ale.

"I hear he was a man of the cloth as well. Fucking bastard, aye," Jamie piped in. "Reckon they'll hang him?"

"Dinna ken, Jamie. Rumour has it there's not enough evidence to hang the bastard. Can ye fucking believe that? I heard they need to find some more evidence, aye. More snuff with poison in it or something. Fuck that, they should just fuckin' hang him."

Geordie sat quietly, thinking of the evidence currently inside a dirty sock under his bed next to the knife. Evidence or not, this could be his easy way out, although four or five days had passed and no police officers had come to talk to him. Maybe he had scared McNabb off. But what about McKeany? Shit, when he'd read about his wife and her cousin he could have fucking howled in the street. How could he have been so fucking *stupid*? The phrase, "biting the hand that feeds you" couldn't have been more fucking apt. He was beginning to think that despite all his education and reading, McKeany still hadn't put two and two together. And if he kept his mouth shut maybe, just maybe, Geordie would stay in the clear. The outhouse was empty of bodies after all. McKeany's note came to mind: "Geordie, bodies are low."

At the time it was a trigger, a demand to refresh stocks. Now, on hindsight, it was a piece of luck that was beyond belief. No bodies, no evidence, right? Damn it, if only that bloody McNabb hadn't seen him with that fucking wheelbarrow. But what could he do now? With Burke's neck snapped and Wilson's about to snap, would his head manage to remain on his shoulders? Of course it damn would. Even if he had to use the goddamn tobacco pouch under his bed, there was no way his body and head would be separated from each other with an audience of many hurtling shite at him before the hangman did what he was paid so little for. *Damn, damn, damn.*

"Shocking, eh, Geordie?"

"Eh? Yeah, aye. Shocking."

Geordie had no idea what was shocking. Rosie could have come back from the dead and shoved her decaying tits in his face.

Greg and Jamie looked at each other again. Something was definitely not right. And when things were *wrong* with Geordie Mill they usually knew about it. Hell, the world knew about it. Greg tried once more.

"Did you see the snuff killer getting a kickin'? I'm surprised ye weren't there, Geordie, you're usually involved."

Greg expected a reaction; a punch, a curse or a kick, but there was nothing. Not even a fist slamming against the table. Geordie Mill finished his drink, belched, stood up and left the tavern without a by your leave. He just walked, leaving Donald McGregor and James Jeffrey completely lost for words.

*

Geordie Mill sat slumped in the wooden chair next to his bed, the pouch of contaminated tobacco resting on his pillow. He'd hoped the ale would settle his dancing mind, but if anything it had made it more restless. Geordie Mill was not one to look back and reflect but he assumed this is what people meant when they said your life flashes in front of your eyes. In this case, though, it was less of a flash and more of a stumble. He couldn't shake the image of his body dangling as the noose gripped his neck. He could see the crowd in the square cheering and jeering at the sight of another murderer getting taken from the world. Rotten fruit would smash into his head, and his last thought would be something along the lines of whether the decaying tomato or apple chucked by the squealing housewife would hit or miss him. No, surely a bag of snuff in the comfort of his own home would be a better way to go. He thought back to Lochee, to the time just after his father took the beating of his life. This is when he'd scavenged like a rat for him and his mother. She had insisted, though, that she needed a man – no matter how hairy, smelly or animal like - she needed someone to look after her and her son.

"You're too young to understand," she'd told Geordie. "It isn't a case of family, it's a case of survival."

He remembered walking into the house to the sight of his mum bent across the table like a mangy dog, with a big, greasy dockworker standing over her, his breeches down to his ankles. It was then that Geordie knew his mother was weak. They *all* were. He was alone in this world and by God he would conquer it. Unlike his weak-willed mother or his loud-mouthed father. Geordie Mill would do *more* than survive. He would *fucking* conquer. He'd steal from the scavengers who lived on their knees and break into people's homes. He'd take just enough to live on without causing suspicion: sideswiping fruit from the markets, going on pick-pocketing sprees in the Nethergate. He'd learn to play, learn to fight and learn to run. He'd teach himself sleight-of-hand card tricks for playing eastern European sailors and master how to steal coins from the boots of street women while fucking them.

Mill thought of all the times he hadn't been as strong, as wiley or as fierce. He recalled his adventures down in Edinburgh five years ago, when his experiences, in hindsight, had made him the force to be reckoned with he was now.

He thought of how hard he'd grafted to get those damn bodies for McKeany. Fuck it, he'd *made* the doctor. He'd also shown that fat whore Rosie who was in charge. Who the *fuck* was she to blackmail him? Bitch. And as for her cheap, skinny slag of a friend, well, he'd taught her a lesson all right. He *was* Geordie fucking Mill, and he *wasn't* to be fucked with. Not now, not ever.

So where had it all gone wrong? Fuck it, he knew. He thought of the two girls and how he'd been seen by that nosey bastard, Donald McNabb, but that wasn't the *moment* he'd fucked up. No, it went back further than that, to that damn posh boy. The moment he'd killed that Mulgrew lad was the moment his life had spiralled out of control. Geordie Mill leant over and picked up the pouch. Was it time for him to exit this world on his *own* terms, unlike that poor bastard Burke? He picked up the pouch and placed it in the inside pocket of his jacket. Then he stood up, deciding to walk around Dundee for one last time. He wanted to say his goodbyes to the city that had made him the man he was.

CHAPTER VI

THE SNUFF KILLER might have been captured, but criminal matters in Dundee certainly hadn't waned. A new species of pickpocketer had formed and they were literally slicing through pockets with their blades. Even women and children were members of these gangs. There had been more fights between sailors, a whaling man in Dudhope Crescent had been murdered and a man had admitted to stabbing his wife in a crime of passion. But Dundee's superintendent had requested for both Graham Whyte and Craig Boyd to attend the funeral of Charlotte McKeany. The police were not expecting trouble but the presence of two officers of the law would do no harm. Anyway, he said it would give them a break. Boyd and Whyte both decided, as they stood together at the back of the crowd of mourners, there were better ways to have a rest. *Like fucking dying.*

They could both see the intimidating figure of Doctor Fairborough and next to him the scarecrow-like Doctor McKeany, his shoulders continuing to rise up and down. Graham doubted whether he had stopped crying since the previous week when they had first paid him a visit.

"Grant this mercy, oh Lord, we beseech thee, to thy servant departed, that she may not receive in punishment the requital of her deeds who in desire did keep. She was taken from us by death most horrid. She was but young and full of love and life. Thy will…"

They looked around as the priest continued with his sermon. Rain had begun to fall and the mass of teachers, students and other upstanding members of the community kept their heads bowed in respect, all secretly grateful this had not happened to one of their loved ones.

"…and as the true faith here united her to the company of the faithful, so may thy mercy unite her above to the choirs of angels. Through Jesus Christ our Lord. Amen."

"Amen," the crowd replied in a mumble.

Whyte and Boyd looked up to the sky and walked slowly from the cemetery. They did not speak to each other as they passed its large entrance and didn't have to. They understood each other perfectly by now. They had been mates and now they were partners. But soon they would be back to the former again. They both knew that today would be their last shift.

*

Paul McKeany barely remembered the service *or* the wake. Only fleeting images from the previous day swept through his mind. Kind words, gentle sentiments, the odd touch on his shoulder, a sombre nod of the head. Sentences such as: "If you ever need anything" / "What a shame" / "Don't worry, justice will be served," did nothing to help. The comments were as worthless and meaningless as the world itself. He recalled telling his father-in-law that he would pay him a visit and that they would discuss his profession, his need to *carry on* despite his loss. It was a lie and he knew it. Not even heaven could redeem him now. He didn't know what happened to his partner Geordie Mill and he frankly didn't care. From now on, none of it was his problem at all.

He sat in the jittery carriage as the driver continued to control the horse headed south. McKeany hadn't considered how uncomfortable the trip all the way down to London would be or that he should have something to eat or drink before setting off. All he'd thought about was getting far, far away. Fairborough and his colleagues would wonder what had happened to the former bright light of the school. Maybe even his students would miss him, but none of that mattered. He needed to escape Dundee, escape Scotland itself. He knew he would never escape his guilt, but hoped distance might make it easier to bear. His driver had passed him a newspaper to read. He flicked through it idly and one article grabbed his attention. The press, it seemed, wanted an admission of guilt from Doctor Knox regarding the William Burke hanging. New laws were discussed about anatomy practices and gaol sentences for people who retrieved bodies from suspicious sources. McKeany folded up the paper and stared back out of the window, watching the lights of the north east fade into one another. This one-way journey across the border was set to be a long one.

CHAPTER VII

IF SOMEONE HAD told Geordie he would be visiting a church on his last day on earth he would have laughed in their stupid faces, but his legs were moving and his feet were indeed taking him there. He walked past the brothels and the taverns, past the docks where he could have watched fights and card games, and past the boiling blubber pots and the scavengers. His life had been one big fight, a battle between him and the rest of the world. He'd always come up the winner and by God, he wasn't about to lose the game now. He would say goodbye on his terms. Bow out with a little bit of dignity. There was absolutely no way the world would watch his neck snap, that was for certain. His father may have been a fucking failure and his mother a fucking weakling, but not him. Not Geordie Mill. Noise surrounded him...clanging from the docks, raised sailors' voices, dogs barking, children crying. It made him all the more determined to reach the peaceful sanctuary of the church. Life indeed was full of surprises. Who would have thought it? He finally stopped outside the church, observing its large, stained glass window and intimidating brick arches. He did not belong here but somehow he knew he was welcome. And this time it was not to intimidate someone, show them not to mess with him, but simply to get some peace before his time was up. He *still* didn't believe in God. How could there be a God anywhere near this town? But strangely, to his own mind, he knew this was the right place to be. He wanted silence before it all ended.

Pushing open the large wooden doors, he walked in, his boots echoing through the empty place of prayer. Candles flickered as he observed the large stage and the pews sitting empty in the cold, quiet room. He went to the front row and slumped down, the image of Jesus Christ stared back down at him. Geordie looked at the figure burdened with the large, wooden cross on his back. He knew how he felt. Within this deserted church, Geordie felt the weight of the pouch of tobacco once more. He placed his head in his hands and closed his eyes. For the first time since he was a baby, he began to cry.

*

"It's peaceful isn't it, Mr Mill?"

Geordie slowly raised his face from his hands. He couldn't see anyone.

"Father?"

"Not quite, Mr Mill. He is attending to the grounds. Father Callahan feels the exterior of the church is just as important as the interior. Sometimes when he talks he compares the building to a person. *Both* the inside and outside are as valuable as one another, but some people focus only on the outside while others focus only on the inside. To be a whole person, it's imperative that one focuses on both. That's sometimes not as easy as it sounds, I'll agree. Occasionally, I can't focus on *any* part of me. Faith is required to retrigger this focus."

The voice was quiet and soothing and came from directly behind Geordie. When he craned his neck around he was faced with Donald McNabb. A scarf covered his neck and he was clasping the Bible. Geordie swiftly moved his head forward again so McNabb couldn't see the defeat that was present in his teary eyes. He needed to gather his thoughts and decide what the fuck was going on before he made another stupid move. He didn't have to wait long.

"Sorry, Mr Mill, I was being rude. Sometimes my tongue runs away with me. My name is Mr McNabb, I should have introduced myself sooner."

"I know who you are," Geordie replied. "You've been asking about me."

Geordie kept his face forward and his gaze on Jesus and the wooden cross. Here was a man with the weight of the world on his shoulders.

"Indeed I have," McNabb replied.

Geordie was surprised how calm he sounded. Why wasn't he scared? He damn well should be shitting himself. He was alone in Geordie's company, after all, with no witnesses. But he was calm, serene even.

"You see, I decided to live again. I've been, let's just say, distracted, lonely and sad. I felt my life was coming to an end and I didn't care. Father Callahan told me I needed a focus, a project if you will. You know, to get me back on my feet. Then I looked out of that window and saw you with that wheelbarrow. *That's it*, I thought, *he's stealing that poor doctor's wheelbarrow*. I decided I could solve some crimes, you know, make Dundee a better place. Do some good instead of mopping the streets like some kind of bum."

Geordie twisted his neck around, eyes narrowing, more in confusion than anger. "Wheelbarrow?"

"Aye," McNabb continued in his gentle, slow tone. "Wheelbarrow. Y'ken. Anyway, when I saw the police at the poor bugger's door I thought to myself, *maybe he knew he was vulnerable and stole his wheelbarrow*. Then the idea came to me that maybe you'd been stealing *more* than just a wheelbarrow."

"Meaning what?" Mill asked, anger returning to his face, his tears now halting. McNabb didn't notice the change and continued.

"I thought you may have had the whole lot...spade, pitch-fork, his entire set of gardening equipment. Anyway, I decided to ask around, get your name."

Before Geordie could interrupt, Donald put a hand on Geordie's right shoulder.

"I'm sorry, mate, I really am. I mean, I talked to Father Callahan who told me that I was being overly suspicious and should be concentrating on myself rather than investigating petty crimes. He told me to mind my own business, in other words. He was right and, of course, it turns oot that poor Doctor McKeany has bigger things tae worry aboot than his damn wheelbarrow. I'm guessing you've heard aboot his poor wife?"

"Aye," said Geordie slowly. He continued to look ahead as he slowly digested what he'd just heard. "Poor bastard," he mumbled.

He looked again at the picture of the skinny, bearded man encumbered with the cross. So he hadn't been rumbled for murder after all. A man who needed a purpose had been planning to report him for stealing a wheelbarrow. That was it. *That* was what it all came down to in the end...a *fucking* wheelbarrow.

Geordie nearly laughed himself off the pew. He couldn't *fucking* believe he had nearly succumbed to his end for this.

"I *am* sorry, Mr Mill. I hope you will pardon my curiosity. Now I have realised it is God that I need, and with God I will find peace. I do hope you will forgive me. Do you? Just imagine if I'd turned up at McKeany's to report a missing wheelbarrow after what happened to his poor wife. I would have looked like a right fool."

McNabb laughed to himself nervously and Geordie began to chuckle also, his eyes now tear free. His mind had finally settled and he answered slowly and with as much dignity as he could muster. "Of course I forgive you, mate. You were only doing the right thing. So do you still think I'm a criminal?"

"A *criminal*, Mr Mill? Dear, oh dear. I would *never* go that far. Like I said, I was a bit lost and needed a purpose. And for that I am truly sorry. I mean, *really*? A borrowed wheelbarrow. Like *that* is important, Mr Mill."

Geordie turned his head again to the front of the church. The pulpit looked back at him, the candles continued to flicker and the sun broke through the stained glass window, forcing him to squint. His mind raced. Was *this* a trick? Did this guy know more than he was letting on? Geordie knew this couldn't be the case. Why would you risk exposing yourself in such a manner? The police, no matter how inefficient, would have had him by now. No, this was what it was. Geordie didn't believe in God, but he believed in luck. He was a *lucky bastard* after all.

He stood up slowly, turned around and with a genuine smile shook Donald McNabb's hand. McNabb shook it back.

"I have found God, Mr Mill, and my pathway. If you indeed need it, I hope you do the same."

"Thank you," Geordie said and sat back down in his pew. He realised once again that he, Geordie Mill, card player, fighter, lover and murderer was well and truly in the clear. His cat-like grin took over his whole face as he stared at the stained glass window.

Epilogue

IT WAS FIVE days since Donald had spoken with Geordie Mill. He couldn't explain why he'd feared the man, but now he didn't at all. In fact, Donald saw him for what he was; a hard-working, salt-of-the-earth type of bloke. Okay, he may have borrowed some equipment, so what? Donald was a little embarrassed about his failed detective work. Father Callahan was correct, he *would* rediscover his path in life, not by snooping but by simply being himself. Maybe he would even find love again, someone to share his bed and his heart with. His chat with Geordie had finished up lasting for over half an hour. They'd talked about the docks and the legendary fights between some of the sailors. They'd chatted about the uprising of the young gangs and the new trend in pickpocketing. They'd discussed matters further afield, news of the British Empire's dominance over the oceans and the increased quality of the ales and tea the ships were returning with.

He told Father Callahan all about their exchange.

"Mr McNabb, would you have been capable of a chat like that not two months ago? I think not. You have recovered from your melancholy and I am proud."

Donald left the meeting with a new sense of pride and purpose. He even had a job interview lined up in the Butcher's shop in Lochee. He'd only do a few hours a day to start with, but he had no doubt that his hours would increase and he'd be back to full financial independence by the end of the year. He'd pray soon about the second chance he'd been given, but first he removed the pouch of tobacco that kind gentlemen Geordie Mill had given him and placed a large pinch on the side of his hand. And to think he used to judge books by their covers. He'd accused the rough man of thievery and in return the man had accepted his apology and presented him with a gift. Father Callahan had been right - life was good.

He looked out of his window and took a large sniff of the fine, dry tobacco.

Pete K Mally is the writer and director of *Caffeine Blues*. He can regularly be seen on the London stand-up comedy circuit.

After running many successful comedy nights, Pete has recently finished two solo UK tours. He also appears at many a rock festival.

Printed in Poland
by Amazon Fulfillment
Poland Sp. z o.o., Wrocław